老人與海
The Old Man and the Sea
中英雙語典藏版

恩尼斯特·海明威——著

李毓昭——譯　曾銘祥——圖

晨星出版

導讀

謙遜與驕傲並行的自我追尋

文字工作者　李曉菁

　　已經八十四天，老人桑地亞哥沒有在海上釣到一條魚。男孩馬諾林與老人在露天酒店喝酒時，年輕漁夫們都拿桑地亞哥的失敗當笑柄，認為他的運氣不再，這已經不是老人第一次那麼久沒釣到魚，只有年老的漁夫們為此感到難過，而隨老人出海多次的馬諾林，還固執地相信桑地亞哥一定會再捕到大魚。老人與男孩之間交流微妙的情感，老人教男孩捕魚，與男孩談論棒球，男孩關心老人的飲食、健康和漁貨量，要不是出於父母的命令，男孩不會換到其他船隻捕魚。老人對洋基棒球隊員狄瑪基歐的強大信心與崇拜感染了男孩，對老人，男孩也懷抱相同的崇敬熱情：「而最棒的漁夫，就是你了！」可是老人「一切都很老舊，唯有那對眼睛，顏色和海一樣，充滿頑強和愉悅。」

 意志與大海的搏鬥

　　主人翁雖以老邁甚至失敗者的身分出場，卻充滿被關注的英雄氣質，老人脾氣很好，性格有股莫名的謙虛退讓，他不認為謙抑是件丟臉的事，況且謙虛無損他對自己能力的驕傲：「我也許沒有自己想像的那麼強壯吧，不過，我知道很多訣竅，而且我有決心和毅力。」第八十五天，老人憑經驗判斷，捕大魚的時機來臨，他已經準備好了。

老人與馬林魚的搏鬥帶來第一波高潮，馬林魚強壯又巨大，上鉤後，老人只好讓魚拖著船前進。孤獨蒼茫的大海中，老人與魚展開拉鋸戰。「魚啊！我到死都會一直陪你。」「這條魚也是我的朋友，我從沒見識過這樣的魚。但我終究要殺了牠。」老人一次次與馬林魚對話，此時的大魚不只是老人與海搏鬥後的戰利品，還化成老人的生死之交。然而老人平靜的口吻，卻也為這次勝利擲下不詳的預言，為接下來老人與群鯊的對抗，埋下不安的伏筆。在歸途，馬林魚新鮮的血味在海中擴散開來，引來各路鯊魚輪番攻擊，場場驚心動魄的保衛戰，將老人的對抗心態描寫得淋漓盡致：「我將和牠們搏鬥到死為止。」三天三夜後，疲倦的老人孤獨地回到住所，只帶回十八呎長、毫無用處的魚脊骨，還有被粗繩磨到破皮出血的雙手，悲涼結局卻也符合作者海明威在作品中一再反覆的主題：「勝者一無所取」。

根據海明威的計算，中篇小說《老人與海》(1952) 共有兩萬六千五百三十一個字，故事架構簡單到幾句話就可以說完，然而是什麼樣的魅力讓這本書成為海明威寫作的顛峰，更因此獲得 1954 年的諾貝爾文學獎？

「我要描寫一個真正的老人，一個真正的孩子，真正的大海，一條真正的魚，和許多真正的鯊魚，然而，如果我能使他們足夠逼真，他們也會代表許多其他的事物。」海明威說，而這本充滿象徵的小說，的確為讀者創造許多想像空間，老人試圖超越極限，挑戰不可能的任務，他要對抗的外在敵人是大自然的力量：海與鯊魚都有捉摸不定的氣質，內在敵人則是老人自己的心態：人必定會邁向年老力衰的事實，而馬諾林這個只在小說前後出場，看似輕盈的配角，其實有舉足輕重的地位。當老人在海上漂流，唯一的安慰是想到男孩：「真希望那孩子在這裡」、「如果那個孩子在這裡就好了」。想到孩子，老人的精神又回來了，在心理上，男孩可說是引導老人回到岸上的希望。而小說中老人反覆提到的小獅子，乍看與海洋的主題不相關，卻隱含力量的象徵意義，讓老人支持到底。獅子與孩子，也是存在主義大師尼采在《查拉圖斯特拉如是說》中所提到的，凡人如要超越自我，必定要經歷以下的精神發展階段：先是負重服從的駱駝期，再來是自尊自重的獅子期，最後是充滿熱情與創造力的孩童期。從這方面說來，海明威的寫實主義，已然滲入存在主義的神秘色彩。

與十九世紀梅爾維爾那軀體碩大又殺氣騰騰的《大白鯊》相較，《老人與海》的馬林魚顯得溫和太多：「雄魚在船邊高高地跳到空中，想要看看雌魚在哪裡，然後潛入水中，牠那淡紫色的翅膀，也就是胸鰭，大大地伸展開來，身上一條條淡紫色寬闊的條紋全露了出來。」老人忘不了那次釣起美麗的雌馬林魚，雄魚在船邊徘徊不止，不捨離去的畫面。魚與大海，在老人的眼中，都散發著濃厚人性。在人與自然競逐的海域，老人對海的瞭解帶有浪漫色彩，他腦中的海是永遠的「海娘子」，那是西班牙人的稱呼，把海當成女人來看待，風平浪靜時，是海娘子對人的恩寵；波濤洶湧無法行船時，是海娘子難免的歇斯底里。那女性陰柔的大海，起伏的韻律是平穩的，老人失落、追尋、捕獲、抗爭、失落的過程，彷彿跟著海的節奏而行，海流甚至保護著老人，平安回到住處。

 ## 作品與作者本身

　　除了海與魚的女性陰柔描述、老人死去多年的老婆，還有結尾那個對鯊魚骨架大驚小怪的女士，《老人與海》並沒有真正的女主角。或許可以說，海明威的創作中，女人的身影大多是被忽略的。這現象可以從海明威的成長經歷看出端倪。1899 年，海明威出生在美國伊利諾州的橡樹公園區，那是中產階級社區，住滿如他母親般虔誠保守的基督教徒。母親以專制的方式教育海明威這害羞、敏感的孩子。為了脫離母親的掌控，海明威長大後離開家鄉，選擇當新聞記者，計畫變成他夢想中的人，就是他筆下創造的那些狠角色，而對女人的輕描淡寫或刻意避而不談，透露出母親在創作上的確給他造成影響。

　　作家的職業和經驗往往與他們創造出的意象息息相關。梅爾維爾曾是貨真價實的船夫，因而他的大海讓人無法喘息，充滿殘酷噬殺、不留餘地的面貌；海明威最為人津津樂道的就是他戰地記者的身分，第一線的報導經驗形成他融合新聞報導與文學技巧的獨特文體，他的文體以簡潔著稱，習慣在事件過後，記憶猶新時，快筆寫下故事。像在普羅納度假後，他寫下《太陽依舊上升》；在非洲坦干伊喀國狩獵的經驗，寫成《非洲的青山》；在西班牙內戰時，他在首都馬德里完成《第五縱隊》；馬德里剛淪陷時，《戰地鐘聲》已經動工了。獨特的戰地經歷也提供《太陽依舊上升》（1926）、《戰地春夢》（1929）、《戰地鐘聲》（1940）的靈感來源，這些場面壯闊的長篇戰爭小說，都曾被改編成電影。一次世界大戰後，在史坦（Gertrude Stein）所謂「失落的一代」時代氛圍中，海明威故事場景遍佈歐美非洲：西班牙鬥牛、西班牙內戰、義大利前線、非洲狩獵活動、美國密西根州森林。他創造的角色強壯、勇敢、誠實，有道德潔癖，渾身爆發神秘的陽剛氣息，卻充滿創傷經驗，例如作戰中生殖器受損的性無能者、在被槍斃前潛入河流的逃兵。他們若非被戰爭毀得身心俱敗，即是在虛矯空洞的文明世界中，嚐著殘喘幻滅的滋味，無力對抗時代給他們的失落感。

　　海明威生前最後發表的作品《老人與海》，承接他慣常運用的主題：「人可以被毀滅，但不能被打敗。」小說中不甘被擊敗的老人，似乎是海明威年老的寫照。一九六一年七月二日，海明威用獵槍自殺，結束六十二年的生命。對他死因的臆測頗多，有人說作者不想再為惡疾所苦；有人說得到諾貝爾獎的《老人與海》已是他的創作顛峰，作者無法超越自己，只好毀滅自己。或許正如海明威創造的角色，他強悍勇敢，卻無力面對被戰亂摧毀、價值失落的時代。

　　「牠們把我打敗了，馬諾林，牠們確實把我打敗了！」老人承認自己失敗，男孩反駁：「牠們沒有打敗你，那條魚沒有。」對於老人的成敗，有兩極的探討。老人對捕魚經驗的驕傲，使他一個人走得太遠，讓自己陷入孤立無援的境地，與其說群鯊攻擊馬林魚，不如說攻擊老人的「驕傲」，這是驕者必敗的道德式解讀法；而在基督教義詮釋下，老人轉化成受難者的象徵，也就是耶穌的角色，老人手上的傷口和回岸後背負桅杆的模樣，與耶穌被釘上十字架雙手流血的姿態有神秘的聯繫。作為人子、耶穌的門徒，苦難是必經的歷程，老人承受的苦難可以滌清肉體帶來的原罪，最後贏得的是精神與意志上的勝利。

老人與海

　　他是個老人，獨自划著小船，在墨西哥灣流中捕魚。已經過了八十四天，他一條魚也沒有捕到。在頭四十天裡，有個男孩跟著他，可是四十天都沒有捕到魚，男孩的父母對孩子說，這老人根本就是個「撒拉歐」（salao），意思是運氣衰到了極點。男孩因此聽從父母的吩咐，上了另一艘船，結果出海頭一星期就捕到了三條大魚。男孩看到老人每天空著船回來都很難過，總是會下去岸邊幫他扛一卷卷的釣索和魚鉤、魚叉，或是從桅杆上卸下來的船帆。船帆布滿了用麵粉袋打的補丁，捲起來時就像一面象徵永遠敗北的旗幟。

　　老人消瘦憔悴，頸後有深深的皺紋。熱帶海洋反射的陽光，在他臉頰的皮膚上留下無傷大雅的褐色癌斑。褐斑沿著雙頰往下蔓延，他的雙手也因為長期操縱釣索釣大魚，而刻畫出一條條傷疤。可是，沒有一條傷疤是新的，那些傷疤和無魚棲生的沙漠所承受的侵蝕一樣古老。

　　他身上的一切都已衰老，唯有那對眼睛，依然像海洋般湛藍且堅定。

　　小船拖上來以後，男孩和老人爬上岸邊。男孩對老人說：「桑地亞哥，我可以再跟你去捕魚了。我們家賺了些錢。」

　　老人教過男孩怎麼捕魚，所以男孩很敬愛他。

　　「不行，」老人說，「你上的那艘船運氣很好，你就待在那裡。」

　　「可是你記得吧，有一次你連續八十七天都沒有捕到魚，不過接下來的三個星期，我們每天都捕到大魚？」

　　「記得，」老人回答，「我知道你不是對我沒信心才離開我的。」

　　「是爸爸要我離開的。我是小孩子，不能不聽他的話。」

　　「我知道，」老人說，「那是難免的。」

　　「爸爸沒什麼信心。」

　　「他沒有，」老人說，「可是我們有，對不對？」

　　「對！」男孩說，「我請你去露天酒吧喝杯啤酒，再把這些東西拿回家，可以嗎？」

　　「有什麼不可以？」老人說，「都是打魚人。」

　　他們在露天酒吧坐了下來，許多漁夫拿老人開玩笑，老人都沒有生氣。有一些比較年長的漁夫只是看著他，為他感到難過。不過他們並沒有表現出來，而是斯文地談論海潮和放魚線的深度、近來持續的好天氣，以及所見所聞。當天有收穫的漁夫早就進來坐了，他們已經把捕到的馬林魚剖開，攤平放在兩塊木板上，兩個人各抬一邊，搖搖晃晃地送到漁會，在那裡等著冷凍卡車把漁獲運到哈瓦那的市場。捕到鯊魚的漁夫則是把鯊魚送到海灣另一邊的鯊魚工廠，那裡的工人會把鯊魚用滑輪吊起來，然後取肝割鰭，再剝下皮，把肉切成條狀，以便用鹽醃起來。

　　風從東方吹來時，會有一股臭味從鯊魚工廠飄到港口：可是今天只有微微的腥味，因為風向轉回北方，而且不久就平息了，露天酒吧上很舒服，陽光普照。

「桑地亞哥。」男孩說。

「什麼事？」老人回答。他拿著酒杯，心裡想著許多陳年往事。

「我去給你弄一些明天用的沙丁魚，好嗎？」

「不用了，你去玩棒球吧。我還可以划船，而且羅黑里奧會幫我撒網。」

「我想去。如果不能和你一起捕魚，至少也要幫你做一些事。」

「你請我喝啤酒了，」老人說，「你是個大人了。」

「你第一次帶我上船時，我幾歲？」

「五歲，那時我釣到一隻魚，因為太早收線，魚差點把船撞成碎片，害你差點沒命。你還記得嗎？」

「我記得魚尾巴砰砰地拍打著，把船板都弄斷了，還有你用木棍打牠的聲音。你把我丟到船頭，那裡堆著一些溼淋

淋的釣索，我覺得整艘船都在晃動，而你用木棍打魚的聲音好像在砍樹，我渾身都是甜甜的血腥味。」

「你真的記得那麼清楚，還是我不久前告訴過你？」

「從我們第一次一起出海起，所有事我都記得。」

老人被太陽曬傷的雙眼，充滿憐愛地看著男孩。

「如果你是我的孩子，我就會帶你去碰碰運氣，」他說，「可是你是你爸爸和你媽媽的孩子，你搭上的船又很幸運。」

「我去拿沙丁魚好嗎？我知道有個地方可以弄到四條魚餌。」

「我今天還有剩，就放在盒子裡，用鹽醃著。」

「讓我去弄四條新鮮的來吧！」

「一條就好。」老人說。他的希望和信心從來不曾消失。而現在，希望和信心更如同吹起的和風一般清新煥發。

「兩條！」男孩說。

「那就兩條吧。」老人同意了。「你不會去偷吧？」

「我敢偷，」男孩說，「可是那是我買來的。」

「謝謝你。」老人說。他太單純了，從來都不去想自己是什麼時候變得這麼謙遜。可是他知道自己早就學會了謙遜，也知道謙遜並不丟臉，不會損害到真正的自尊。

「從海潮來看，明天會是好天氣。」

「你打算去哪裡？」男孩問。

「夠遠的地方，等風轉向時回得來就好了。我要在天亮以前出發。」

「我會盡量叫船主去遠一點，」男孩說，「如果你釣到什麼大魚，我們就可以過去幫你。」

「他不喜歡去太遠的地方捕魚。」

「他是不喜歡，」男孩說，「可是有的東西我看得見，他卻看不見，譬如看到有鳥在抓魚，我就會叫他去追海豚。」

「他的眼睛這麼差嗎？」

「他都快瞎了。」

「真奇怪，」老人說，「他從來沒有捕過海龜，那才真的傷眼力呢！」

「可是你在莫斯基托海岸捕了那麼多年的海龜，你的眼睛還是很好。」

「我是個奇怪的老頭子。」

「但你現在還有力氣應付真正的大魚嗎？」

「我想沒問題，而且我懂得很多訣竅。」

「我們把這些東西帶回家吧，」男孩說，「這樣我才能去拿魚網，再去弄沙丁魚。」

他們從船上取出漁具。老人肩挑著桅杆，男孩抱著木箱，裡面裝著捲得緊緊的棕色釣索、魚鉤和帶柄的魚叉。裝釣餌的盒子放在船尾底下，木棍也放在那裡，用來制伏已拖到船邊的大魚。沒有人會偷老人的東西，可是把帆和沉重的釣索帶回家比較好，因為露水會把那些東西泡壞。雖然老人確定當地人不會偷他的東西，但是他認為把魚鉤和魚叉留在船上是不必要的誘惑。

他們沿著馬路往上走，來到老人的小屋，從敞開的門進去。老人把捲著帆的桅杆靠在牆上，男孩就把箱子和其他器具放在桅杆的旁邊，桅杆幾乎和屋裡唯一的房間一樣長。小屋是用本地人稱為「古阿諾」(guano) 的棕櫚樹堅硬的葉鞘搭建的，裡面有一張床、一張桌子、一把椅子，泥地上有個地方可以燒炭煮飯。棕色的牆壁是把纖維強韌的棕櫚樹葉壓平後編織而成，上面掛著彩色的基督聖心像，還有一幅柯布雷的聖母像。這些都是他妻子的遺物，以前牆上還掛著他妻子的彩色照片，但是他把它拿下來了，因為看到它會感到格

外寂寞。現在那張照片放在角落的架子上，就在乾淨的襯衫底下。

「你有什麼吃的？」男孩問。

「一鍋魚肉黃米飯，你要不要來一點？」

「不了，我要回家吃。要不要我幫你生火？」

「不用，我待會兒再弄，也許我會吃冷飯。」

「我可以拿走魚網嗎？」

「當然可以。」

屋子裡根本沒有魚網，男孩記得他們早就把魚網賣了。可是他們每天都假裝有這回事。男孩也知道，這裡也沒有什麼魚肉黃米飯。

「八十五是個幸運數字，」老人說，「想不想看到我拖一條一千多磅的魚回來？」

「我去拿魚網，然後去弄沙丁魚來。你就坐在門口曬太陽好嗎？」

「好，我有昨天的報紙，可以看看棒球新聞。」

昨天的報紙是否也是捏造的，男孩不知道。可是老人從床底下找出了報紙。

「佩利可在酒吧給我的。」他解釋。

「我拿到沙丁魚就回來，我會把你的和我的都冰起來，明天早上就可以分著用。我回來時，你可以告訴我球賽的消息。」

「洋基隊不能輸。」

「可是我擔心克利夫蘭的印地安人隊太強了。」

「對洋基隊要有信心啊，孩子！想一想了不起的狄馬吉奧。」

「我擔心底特律老虎隊和克利夫蘭印地安人隊都會贏。」

「小心一點，不然你連辛辛那提紅人隊和芝加哥白襪隊都要擔心了。」

「你仔細看，等我回來再告訴我。」

「你看我們該不該買一張尾碼是八十五的彩券？明天是第八十五天了。」

「可以呀，」男孩說，「可是怎麼不照你那八十七天的最高記錄買？」

「同樣事情不會發生第二遍。你看能不能找到八十五號的彩券？」

「我可以買到一張。」

「一張就好。需要兩塊半，我們可以跟誰借？」

「那很容易，我隨時都借得到兩塊半。」

「我想我可能也借得到，可是我盡量不要去借。你一開始借，接下來就要乞討了。」

「老伯要穿暖和點，」男孩說，「要知道現在是九月了。」

「正是大魚來的月分，」老人說，「五月時，每個人都能當漁夫。」

「我現在就去拿沙丁魚。」男孩說。

男孩回來時，老人已經在椅子上睡著了，而太陽也已西下。男孩把床上的舊軍毯拿下來，連著椅背圍住老人的肩膀。他的肩膀很奇怪，雖然很老了，卻還是很強健，就像他的頸子，仍然很硬朗。老人睡著時頭往前垂落，使得頸後的皺紋並沒有那麼明顯。他的襯衫和船帆一樣滿是補丁，日曬使得它的顏色褪得深淺不一。然而，老人的頭顯得非常衰老，閉著眼睛，臉上毫無生氣。報紙攤在他的膝蓋上，被手臂的重量壓住，才沒有被晚風吹走。他的雙腳是赤裸的。

男孩離開了一會兒，再回來時，老人還在熟睡。

「老伯，醒醒。」男孩說，把一隻手放在老人的膝蓋上。

老人張開眼睛，過了好一陣子才醒轉過來。然後他露出微笑。

「你帶了什麼來了？」他問。

「晚餐，」男孩說。「我們來吃晚餐。」

「我不太餓。」

「來吃啦，你不吃東西是不能捕魚的。」

「我這麼做過。」老人說著，站起來，把報紙折好，再開始摺毛毯。

「把毛毯披在身上吧，」男孩說，「只要我還活著，你就不能空著肚子去捕魚。」

「那麼你要活很久，好好照顧你自己，」老人說，「我們要吃什麼？」

「黑豆、米飯、炸香蕉，還有一點燉肉。」

男孩把食物放在雙層的金屬容器裡，從露天酒吧提回來。他的口袋還塞著兩副刀叉和湯匙，每副都用紙巾裹著。

「這是誰給你的？」

「老闆馬丁。」

「我得謝謝他。」

「我已經謝過他了，」男孩說，「你不必再去謝他。」

「捕到大魚，我要把肚子的肉給他，」老人說，「他這樣對我們，可不只這一次吧？」

「我想是的。」

「不只是肚子的肉，我還得給他別的。他對我們太好了。」

「他還給我兩瓶啤酒。」

「我最喜歡罐裝啤酒了。」

「我知道，可是這是瓶裝的，阿特威啤酒，我會把瓶子還回去。」

「你真好，」老人說，「可以開動了吧？」

「我早就要你開動了，」男孩對老人柔聲說著。「我要等你準備好了，才打開飯盒。」

「我準備好了，」老人說，「我只是要花點時間洗手。」

你要在哪裡洗手？男孩心想。村裡的自來水要到下兩條街才有。我應該幫他提些水過來，男孩心想，還要肥皂和好毛巾。我怎麼這麼粗心呢？我還得給他弄件襯衫和外套過

冬，再來雙像樣的鞋子，外加一條毛毯。

「你的燉肉真好吃。」老人說。

「告訴我球賽的消息。」男孩央求他。

「就像我之前說的，美國聯盟裡面只有洋基隊夠看。」老人愉快地說。

「他們今天輸了。」男孩告訴他。

「那不算什麼，了不起的狄馬吉奧，恢復了以前的身手。」

「洋基隊裡還有其他人啊！」

「話是沒有錯，可是有他就不一樣了。在另一個聯盟中，如果要問布魯克林和費城這兩支球隊哪支比較強，我會說是布魯克林隊。這麼一說，我又想到了費城的狄克‧西斯勒在老球場的精采打擊。」

「沒有人的打擊像他那麼棒，他擊出來的球是我看過最遠的。」

「記得他以前常常去露天酒吧嗎？我很想帶他去捕魚，可是我膽子太小了，不敢跟他說，結果叫你去問他，你也不敢去。」

「我記得，那真是大錯特錯。他說不定會跟我們去，這樣，我們就可以一輩子回味這件事了。」

「我希望能夠帶了不起的狄馬吉奧去捕魚，」老人說，「聽說他父親是個漁夫，或許他以前也像我們現在一樣窮，能夠了解我們的心意。」

「那了不起的西斯勒的父親從來沒有窮過，他父親在我這個年紀時，已經在打大聯盟了。」

「我在你這個年紀時，在一艘跑非洲的方帆船上當水手，到了晚上，可以在沙灘上看到獅子。」

「我知道，你跟我說過。」

「我們是要談非洲還是棒球？」

「我想棒球好了，」男孩說，「告訴我了不起的約翰‧Ｊ‧馬格羅的事情。」他照西班牙語把Ｊ唸成「霍塔」。

「很久以前，他也常去露天酒吧，可是一喝了酒，就會變得很粗暴，說話刻薄，很難相處。他念念不忘的就是賽馬和棒球，至少他總是會把賽馬的名單放在口袋裡，講電話時也經常提到馬的名字。」

「他是個了不起的球隊經理，」男孩說，「我父親認為他是最了不起的。」

「那是因為他經常來這裡，」老人說，「如果杜洛喬每一年都來這裡，你父親也會說他是最了不起的經理。」

「那誰才是最了不起的經理？路克，還是邁克‧供札列？」

「我想這兩個人都差不多。」

「而最棒的漁夫就是你了！」

「不是，我知道有些人比我好。」

「才不是呢，」男孩說，「好的漁夫是很多，有些也相當了不起，可是只有你是最棒的！」

「謝謝你，你讓我好開心。但願不會出現一隻太大的魚，證明我們兩個都錯了。」

「如果你仍然像你所說的那麼強壯，就不會有那種魚出現。」

「我可能沒有自己所想的那麼強壯，」老人說，「可是我懂很多訣竅，而且我有決心。」

「你現在該去睡覺了，這樣明天早上才會有精神，我會把這些東西送回露天酒吧。」

「那就晚安了，我一早就會叫醒你。」

「你是我的鬧鐘。」男孩說。

「年齡是我的鬧鐘，」老人說，「為什麼老年人都會醒得那麼早？難道是要讓他的一天長一點？」

「我不知道，」男孩說，「我只知道小伙子都很貪睡，而且睡得很沉。」

「我會記得的，」老人說，「到時候我會去叫你。」

「我不喜歡由船主來叫醒我，那會顯得我不如他。」

「我了解。」

「老伯好好睡。」

男孩離開了。他們在沒有燈的桌邊吃完晚飯，老人就脫下長褲，摸黑上床。他捲起長褲，把報紙塞在裡面當枕頭，然後用毛毯把自己裹起來，睡在舖滿舊報紙的彈簧床上。

他很快就睡著了，夢見小時候去過的非洲，那裡有長長的金色和白色沙灘，白得刺眼，還有陡峭的海岬和高大的褐

色山脈。如今他每天夜裡都回到那條海岸邊，在夢中聽見波濤的怒吼，看到當地人的船隻破浪而來。他在沉睡中聞到甲板的焦油和填縫隙的麻絮味，也聞到了清晨的微風從陸地吹過來的非洲氣息。

通常一聞到陸上的微風氣息，他就會醒過來，穿好衣服，去叫醒男孩。可是今晚陸上的微風氣息來得太早了，他在夢中知道時間還早，就繼續做夢，看到島上的白色山峰從海上升起，然後又夢到卡那利群島的幾個港口和停泊處。

他早就不再夢到暴風雨，不再夢見女人和重大事件，也沒有大魚、打架、比腕力，也不再夢見妻子了。他現在只會夢見許多地方和沙灘上的獅子。那些獅子跟小貓一樣在暮色中嬉戲，他愛那些獅子就像他愛那個男孩，但他從來沒有夢見過男孩。他只是會醒過來，從敞開的門望一望月亮，然後攤開捲起的長褲並穿上。他走到屋外小便，再沿路往下走，去叫醒那個男孩。他在清晨的寒氣中顫抖，可是他知道再抖一陣子就會逐漸暖和，何況他馬上就要划槳了。

男孩的家門沒有上鎖，他把門打開，踩著赤腳悄悄走進去。男孩在頭一間臥房的小床上熟睡，漸趨黯淡的月光透了進來，老人可以清楚看到他。他輕輕握住男孩的一隻腳，直到男孩醒過來轉身看他，他才鬆手。老人點點頭，男孩就從床邊的椅子上拿起長褲，坐在床上，把褲子穿上去。

老人走到門外，男孩跟隨在後，仍然睡眼惺忪。老人把手臂搭在他的肩膀上說：「抱歉。」

「怎麼會，」男孩說，「男人就應該這樣。」

他們順著路走，來到老人的小屋。沿路上，在黑暗中，有些赤著腳的人影在晃動，扛著他們船上的桅杆。

來到老人的小屋時，男孩拿起籃中的多捲釣索和魚叉、魚鉤，老人把捲著帆的桅杆扛在肩上。

「你要喝咖啡嗎？」男孩問。

「我們先把用具拿到船上再去喝。」

他們在專為大清早起床工作的漁夫開設的攤子上，喝著煉乳罐裡的咖啡。

「老伯睡得怎樣？」男孩問。雖然要把睡蟲驅散還是很困難，可是他現在已經清醒了。

「太好了，馬諾林，」老人說，「我今天很有把握。」

「我也是。」男孩說，「我這就去拿我們的沙丁魚，還有你的新鮮釣餌。那個船主都自己搬船上的用具，不給別人碰任何東西。」

「我們不一樣，」老人說，「你五歲的時候，我就讓你搬東西了。」

「我知道，」男孩說，「我馬上就回來。再喝一杯咖啡吧，我們在這裡可以賒帳。」

他走開了，光腳踩著珊瑚礁石，前往存放魚餌的冰庫。

老人慢慢喝著咖啡，這會是他整天唯一下肚的東西，他知道他應該喝下去。很久以前，他就對吃感到厭倦，所

以從來不帶午餐。船頭有一瓶清水，他一整天有那樣東西就夠了。

現在男孩回來了，帶著沙丁魚和兩個用報紙包裹的釣餌。他們順著小路走下去，踩著布滿卵石的沙灘，來到小船旁邊。他們抬起小船，讓它滑進水中。

「老伯，祝你好運！」

「祝你好運！」老人說。他把槳上的繩圈套在槳栓上，槳在水中一戳，身體往前傾，開始在黑暗中划出港口。這時也有其他船從別的沙灘出海，雖然現在月亮沉到山後面去了，老人看不見，卻聽得到他們划槳的潑刺聲。

有時候會有人在某艘船上說話，不過大部分的船除了划槳聲之外，都是沉默無聲。他們一離開港口就分散開來，每艘都朝著各自期望能捕到魚的海洋彼方前進。老人知道自己划得很遠了，把陸地的氣息拋在後頭，划進海洋在日出時的清新氣息中。他划過漁人稱為「大井」的海域時，看到墨西哥海草在水中發出的粼光，因為那裡有個陡降七百噚[1]的深淵，海流沖擊海底峭壁時形成漩渦，使各種各樣的魚類在那裡聚集。那裡有一群群蝦子和可當釣餌的魚，最深的洞穴裡，有時還會有成群的烏賊。這些生物會在夜晚游到接近水面的地方，被漫游海中的大魚取食。

黑暗中，老人感覺得到黎明已近，他划著槳，聽到飛魚

1. 噚：1 噚等於 6 呎或是 1.8288 公尺。

跳離水面的顫音，還有牠們在黑暗中飛走時，僵直的翅膀發出的嘶嘶聲響。他很喜愛飛魚，因為那是他在海洋中最好的朋友。他同情鳥兒，特別是纖細黝黑的小燕鷗，牠們總是飛來飛去，尋尋覓覓，卻幾乎一無所獲。他覺得，鳥的生活比人類還辛苦，除了專門打劫的鳥和體型壯碩的鳥以外。他想：「為什麼要把鳥類創造得這麼纖細弱小，像海燕那樣，而海洋卻是如此的殘酷？海洋是和善美麗的，可是她也會變得非常殘酷，而且說變就變，那些飛鳥卻必須潛入水中覓食，發出細小的哀鳴，在這樣的海上顯得太纖弱了。」

他總是把大海稱為「海娘子」，那是西班牙人對她的暱稱。愛海的人有時候會咒罵她，可是總是把她看成一個女人。那些年輕的漁夫用浮標當作釣索的浮子，賣鯊魚肝臟賺了大錢，就買來小汽艇，把海洋叫做陽性的「海郎兒」。他們提到海洋時，把她當成了一個競爭對手或一個地方，甚至是一個敵人。可是老人總是把海洋當成女性，她有時會對他施恩，有時則拒絕施恩，而如果她的舉止狂暴或邪惡，那也是因為她身不由己。月亮會影響她，就像會影響女人一樣，他想。

他穩定地划著槳，一點都不費力，因為他保持一定的速度，而且除了偶爾海流會激起漩渦之外，海面平靜無波。他讓海流為他做三分之一的工作，因而在天快亮時，他發現自己的位置已經比原先所預期的遠。

他心想，我在這海底的深淵上耗了一個星期，卻沒有半點收穫。今天我要到鰹魚和長鰭鮪魚成群出沒的地方，也許那兒會有一條大魚。

天色還沒有全亮，他就把餌拿出來，讓它隨著海潮漂浮。第一個餌垂到四十噚深，第二個是七十五噚，第三個和第四個分別下垂到一百噚和一百二十五噚深的藍色海洋中。每個餌頭都是朝下的，鉤子上端包在魚餌裡面，綁得緊緊的，鉤子所有突出來的部分，像是彎曲和尖刺，都用新鮮的沙丁魚裹著。每隻沙丁魚的雙眼都被鉤子穿過去，使突出來的金屬變成半圓的花環狀。整個釣鉤都會讓大魚覺得香甜可口。

男孩給了他兩隻新鮮的小鮪魚，或稱為長鰭鮪魚，像秤錘一樣懸在兩條最深的釣索上。另外兩條釣索則是掛著一隻藍色金鰺和一隻巴氏若鰺，他先前就用過這兩隻魚了，可是還很完整，何況有鮮美的沙丁魚增添風味和吸引力。每一條釣索都像大枝鉛筆那麼粗，一端結成環狀，繫在從樹上扯下來的小枝上，魚餌一被觸動或拉動，樹枝就會下沉，而每一條釣索都有兩捲四十噚長，能與其他的備用捲軸連接，必要時可以讓魚拖出最長達三百噚的釣索。

現在，老人盯著小船邊的三根樹枝在水裡浮沉，他緩緩搖著槳，使釣索保持筆直和垂落的深度。天色已經很亮了，太陽隨時都會升起。

老人與海

　　太陽微微從海上升起，老人看到其他船隻低低伏在水面上，船頭朝向海岸，隨著潮水散布開來。太陽變得更明亮了，水面上波光閃爍。過了一會兒，太陽升得更高，平靜的海面使陽光反射到老人的眼中，刺眼得讓他划槳時要避開太陽。他朝水裡望了望，看到釣索一直垂到漆黑的海底。他把釣索維持得比別人還直，這樣，在漆黑的每一層水流中，都會有一個餌在他希望的位置上等待游過的魚兒。其他漁夫都是讓魚餌隨著海流浮動，有時候魚餌只有六十噚深，他們卻以為有一百噚。

　　可是，他心裡想著，我下餌一向都很精準，只可惜運氣不好。但是，誰知道呢？也許今天就轉運了。每一天都是新的開始，有好運道當然不錯，可是我寧可做到分毫不差，這樣，運氣來的時候，你就有所準備了。

　　兩個小時過去了，太陽升得更高了，他朝東邊望時不再那麼刺眼了。視線所及之處只有三艘船，在遠遠的海岸邊，看起來十分低矮。

　　他心想，我這輩子都被朝陽刺痛眼睛。不過，到現在我的眼睛還很好，即使在傍晚直視太陽，眼前也不會發黑。雖然傍晚的陽光更為強烈，早晨的陽光卻令人難受。

　　這時，他看到了一隻軍艦鳥，伸展長長的黑翅，在他前面的天空盤旋。他倏地俯衝，翅膀傾斜後縮，然後再度盤旋。

　　「牠一定是看到什麼了，」老人大叫。「那樣子不像只是看看而已！」

他緩慢而穩定地划向軍艦鳥盤旋的地方，不慌不忙，讓釣索保持筆直下垂，但又稍微緊靠著海流，這麼一來他依然循著正確的方法捕魚，卻又比不利用鳥兒引路時的速度來得快。

鳥兒在空中飛得更高了，而且再度盤旋，翅膀一動也不動。接著牠猛然下墜，老人看到飛魚躍出海面，拚命在水面上游。

「海豚！」老人大叫，「大海豚！」他擱下船槳，從船頭下面拿起一條細釣索。釣索接著一根鐵絲和中型魚鉤，他拿一隻沙丁魚餌掛在鉤子上，從船邊把釣索放下去，然後綁在船尾的圓形螺栓上。他接著在另一條釣索上裝魚餌，把線捲起來，放在船頭的陰影處。他回過身去，一面划船，一面觀察那隻長翅黑鳥，牠正在水面上低飛，忙著搜索食物。

　　就在他觀察時，那隻鳥再度下墜，斜著翅膀潛水追逐飛魚，牠猛烈地拍擊雙翅，卻徒勞無功。老人看到大海豚追趕四處逃竄的魚群時，在水中掀起微微的水波。海豚在躍起的飛魚下面破水而行，急速地游動，想要在魚落下時接個正著。他想，那是一大群海豚，散得很開，飛魚存活的希望很渺茫。而鳥兒也沒有機會逮到魚，因為飛魚的體形對牠而言太大，速度也太快了。

　　他望著飛魚一次又一次地跳躍，還有鳥兒毫無收穫的舉動。他想，那群海豚應該已經離開我了，牠們游得又快又遠。可是，也許我可以抓到一隻落單的，也許我的大魚就在牠們旁邊。我的大魚一定在某個地方。

　　陸地上空的雲像山脈一樣高高升起，海岸形成長長的綠線，後方是灰藍色的山丘。現在的海水是暗藍色的，暗得發紫。他低下頭，看到紅色的浮游生物在幽暗的水中飄浮，太陽在底下製造出怪異的亮光。他看看釣索，每一條都筆直垂到水裡看不見的地方。他很高興看到這麼多浮游生物，因為那表示這裡有魚。太陽懸得更高了，它在水裡產生的怪異亮光意味著好天氣，陸地上空的雲彩形狀也指出了這一點。可是幾乎已經看不見那隻鳥了，水面上也沒有什麼東西，除了幾塊被太陽曬得褪色的黃色馬尾藻之外，就只有一隻紫色的葡萄牙戰艦──僧帽水母──牠色彩斑斕的身形很完整，有著膠質的氣囊，浮在小船的近旁。牠翻了個身，再擺正姿勢，就像個氣泡一樣輕巧地飄浮著，後面長著有毒的紫色觸鬚，在水裡拖了一碼長。

「毒汁，」老人說，「你這婊子養的！」

他輕輕搖著槳，俯視海水，看到小魚，在水母觸鬚產生的氣泡影子下游動著，像是被觸鬚的色彩染上般。水母的毒素對牠們不起作用，人就不一樣了。老人釣魚時，釣索有時候會纏到這種黏滑的紫色觸鬚，他的手臂和手掌就會又腫又痛，就像碰到有毒的長春藤或橡樹。可是這種毒汁發作得很快，像是被鞭子抽打一般猛然襲來。

閃閃發光的氣泡很美，可是那是海裡面最虛假的東西，老人喜歡看大海龜吃牠們的樣子。海龜看到牠們，就會從正面游過去，然後閉上眼睛，全身縮在甲殼裡，把牠們連觸鬚一起吃掉。老人很愛看海龜吃水母，也很喜歡在暴風雨過後的海灘上踩水母，聽腳底下的老繭踩破牠們的噗噗聲。

他很喜歡綠蠵龜和玳瑁，因為他們動作優雅、敏捷，而且非常值錢，可是他對龐大、愚笨的赤蠵龜則抱以不帶惡意的輕蔑，因為牠們穿著黃色的鎧甲，求愛的方式怪模怪樣，而且還閉著眼睛快樂地吃食僧帽水母。

雖然曾在捕龜船待過很多年，他對海龜並沒有任何神祕的看法。他反而很同情海龜，即使是龜殼和小船一樣長，而且重達一噸的大革龜。大多數人對海龜都很無情，因為海龜的心臟即使切割下來，仍然可以跳動好幾個小時。老人想，我也有那樣的心，而我的四肢也和牠們一樣。他會吃白色的海龜蛋，以增強精力。整個五月他都在吃龜蛋，以便在九月和十月時有力氣捕到真正的大魚。

他每天也會喝一杯鯊魚肝油，漁夫存放用具的小屋子裡有一大桶，誰要喝都可以。大部分的漁夫都很討厭那個味道，可是再怎麼樣也不會比在半夜起床更令人難過，而且鯊魚肝油可以驅寒，對眼睛也很好。

這時，老人抬起頭來，看到那隻鳥又在盤旋了。

「牠找到魚了！」他大聲說著。沒有飛魚躍出水面，也沒有可以做餌的小魚四處逃竄。可是就在老人觀望時，一隻小鮪魚跳到空中，轉個身，頭朝下栽進水中。那隻鮪魚在太陽下閃出銀光，在牠回到水裡之後，又有一隻、再一隻躍起，分往不同的方向跳下，激起水花，跟著小魚做長距離的跳躍。牠們圍著小魚繞圈子，追逐著牠們。

　　老人心想，要不是鮪魚游得那麼快，我就捕得到牠們了。他望著魚群在水裡翻騰，在這同時，那隻鳥兒趁機俯衝，下水捕捉因為驚慌而被逼上水面的小魚。

　　「這隻鳥可幫了大忙。」老人說。就在這時，他腳下連著船尾的那條釣索突然繃緊了，他丟下船槳，抓緊釣索，開始往上拉時，感覺到小鮪魚顫抖的掙扎。他越往上拉，顫抖就越厲害，他看到那隻魚的藍色背脊和金色側邊，然後把牠甩進船裡。牠躺在船尾的陽光下，身體結實，形狀有如子彈，瞪著大而呆滯的眼睛，急速地抖動精巧敏捷的尾巴，拚命撞擊船板。老人出於善意地打牠的頭、踢牠，在船尾的陰影下，牠的身體依然在抖動。

「是長鰭鮪魚！」他大聲說道，「可以做個漂亮的魚餌，大概有十磅重！」

他不記得從什麼時候開始會在一個人時高聲說話。早年身邊沒有人時，他會唱唱歌，有時夜晚一個人在漁船或捕龜船上值班掌舵時，他也會哼哼唱唱。也許是在那男孩離開他，他變得孤單一人時，才開始大聲說話的。可是他不記得了。他和男孩一道捕魚時，通常只在需要時才說話。晚上或是被風雨困住時，他們講得比較多。在海上不講廢話是一種美德，老人總是這麼認為，也謹守這個規矩。可是，現在他想到什麼就會說什麼，反正不會干擾到別人。

「如果有人聽到我大聲說話，他們可能會以為我發瘋了！」他大聲說著。「可是既然我沒有發瘋，我就不在乎。誰像那些闊佬在船上有收音機跟他們講話，還會播棒球賽給他們聽。」

現在可沒有時間去想棒球賽，他心想。現在只有一件事可以想，我生來就是為了幹這件事的。也許有隻大魚在那群魚旁邊，他心想。我從那群捕食的長鰭鮪魚中，只逮到一隻落單的。牠們跑得又快又遠。今天游到水面上來的動作都好快，而且都游向西北方。是現在這個時間正好如此，還是某種我不知道的天氣預兆？

此時已看不見海岸的綠色草木，只能看到頂端泛白的青色山丘，彷彿覆蓋著白雪，而雲層猶如在上面高聳的雪山。海水暗沉，陽光在水中形成七彩的光芒。浮游生物所變幻的

萬點霞光已被高昇的太陽沖淡,而那是老人此時於蔚藍的海域中唯一看得見的深海虹光,他的釣索就在那裡筆直深入一哩深的水中。

鮪魚群又沉下去了。漁夫把這一類的魚都稱為鮪魚,只有在出售或用來換魚餌時,才會去分辨牠們正確的名稱。此時豔陽高照,老人感覺到頸背十分灼熱,划槳時汗水順著他的背直往下淌。他心想,我可以任船漂流,先睡個覺,把釣索套在腳趾上,一有動靜我就會醒過來。可是今天是第八十五天了,我應該好好工作。

就在他望著釣索時,他看到一根樹枝猛然下沉。

「來了,」他說,「來了!」他小心擱下船槳,以免震動船身。他伸出右手去拿釣索,輕輕夾在拇指和食指之間。他感覺不到任何拉力或重量,但還是輕輕握住那條線。然後又來了,這回只是試探性的拉扯,既不認真也沒有用力,他很清楚這是什麼意思。一百噚深的地方有隻馬林魚正在享用覆蓋在鉤尖和鉤柄上的沙丁魚,那個手工製的魚鉤還穿過了一隻小鮪魚的頭。

老人輕巧地握住魚線,

小心地用左手把線從樹枝上解開。現在釣索可以在他的手指中滑動了，那隻魚一點都不會感覺到拉力。

老人心想，離岸邊這麼遠，又在這個月分，一定是條大魚。吃吧，魚兒，吃下去！拜託吃下去。那些魚多麼鮮美啊，你可是在六百呎深的黑暗冷水裡。在黑暗中再轉一圈，然後回來吃完吧！

他感覺到輕微的拉扯，然後是猛烈地一拉，一定有隻沙丁魚頭很難從鉤子上扯下來。接著就沒有動靜了。

「快點，」老人大聲說道。「再轉一圈，聞一聞，不是很美味嗎？現在好好吞下去，還有鮪魚呢，又肥又冰又好吃！別害羞嘛，魚兒，吃下去！」

他把釣索握在拇指和食指之間等待著，除了這條釣索，他同時也留意著別條，因為那條魚可能會上下游動。又來了一道同樣的輕柔拉扯。

「牠會吃的，」老人大聲說道。「老天爺幫幫忙，讓牠吃下去吧！」

然而，牠並沒有吃。牠走了，老人感覺不到任何動靜。

「牠不可能走掉的，」他說，「老天爺知道，牠不會走的。牠會轉個圈，也許牠以前上過鉤，所以想起什麼了。」

他感覺到釣索輕微的觸動，心裡好高興。

「牠剛才在兜圈子，」他說，「他會吃的。」

老人很高興感覺到輕微的拉扯，但接著就是猛烈的拖力，力量大得難以相信。這就是那隻魚的重量。他任由釣索往下滑，不斷地往下滑，兩捲預備釣索已經用完一捲了。釣索在手指間輕輕地往下滑動時，老人感覺得到龐大的重量，雖然手指並沒有捏得很緊。

「好大的一條魚啊！」他說，「牠現在把餌橫啣在嘴裡，拉著它跑。」

老人心想，牠接下來會轉個圈，然後吞下魚餌。他並沒有把這句話說出來，因為他知道，如果你把好事情說出來，事情可能就不會發生了。他知道這是條大魚，想像牠把鮪魚橫啣在嘴裡，在黑暗中游開的模樣。在這一刻，他感覺到牠停了下來，可是重量還在。然後重量增加了，他放出了更多的釣索。他在拇指和食指中使了一點點力，覺得重量更大了，而且在直直往下沉。

「上鉤了，」他說，「現在我得讓牠慢慢吃。」

他讓釣索從手指中滑脫，同時伸出左手，把兩捲備用釣

索的線頭打結，連在另一條釣索的活結上。現在他準備妥當了，除了正在用的這一捲之外，他還有三捲四十噚長的備用釣索。

「再多吃一點，」他說，「很好吃吧！」

他心想，吃下去，那樣子鉤尖才會進入你的心臟，取走你的小命。乖乖浮上來，讓我把魚叉戳到你的身上。好了，你準備好了嗎？你這頓飯吃得夠久了嗎？

「就是現在！」他大聲說著，兩手用力拖，拉回一碼的釣索，再繼續拉，左右手交替拉扯，使出手臂的全部力氣，再用上身體的重量。

一點用也沒有。那條魚慢慢游開了，老人連一吋也無法把牠拉近。他的釣索很強韌，是專用來對付大魚的，他用背部的力量去拖，線繃得好緊，以至於有串串水珠從線上崩落。釣索開始在水中發出拖長的嘶嘶聲，但他還是握得很緊，穩穩坐在船板上，身體往後仰，以抵抗大魚的拉力。小船開始慢慢朝著西北方移動。

那條魚安穩地游著，老人就隨著牠在平靜的水面上緩緩漂移。其他魚餌還在水裡面，但是老人已經顧不了那麼多了。

「真希望那孩子在這裡。」老人大聲說。「我正在被一隻魚拖著走，成了繫繩子的木樁了。我可以把釣索拉緊，可是這樣子牠會把釣索扯斷。我得抓牢牠，牠要多少釣索就給牠多少。感謝上天，牠是在往前游，而不是往下潛。」

如果牠硬要往下潛，我該怎麼辦？我不知道。如果牠突

然潛進水裡死了，我也不知道該怎麼辦。可是我會想想辦法，有很多辦法可以想的。

他用背抵住釣索，看看它在水裡的斜度。小船穩定地朝西北方移動。

這樣會要了牠的命，老人心想。牠不可能這樣永遠撐下去。可是四個小時過後，這條魚仍然拖著小船，穩穩地往外海游去，而老人也依舊堅定地握著繞過背脊的釣索。

「我是在中午釣到牠的，」他說，「到現在我連牠的影子都沒看到。」

還沒有釣到魚之前，他一直把頭上的草帽往下壓，現在額頭被帽子刺得好痛。他的口也渴了，他彎下膝蓋，小心避免觸到釣索，盡可能移到船頭，用一隻手去取水瓶。他打開瓶子，喝了一點點，然後靠在船頭上休息。他坐在沒有裝在桅座上的桅杆和風帆上，盡量不去想，只是忍耐著。

他回過頭去看，發現陸地消失了。沒有關係，我可以靠著哈瓦那的燈光回去，他心想。離太陽下山還有兩個小時，也許牠會在天黑以前浮出來。如果沒有，也許牠會和月亮一起現身。如果還是沒有，也許牠會和日出一起上來。我沒有抽筋，身體也很強壯。何況嘴裡有鉤子的是牠。可是那隻魚真是厲害，可以這樣拖著船跑。牠一定是唧著釣索，閉緊了嘴巴。真希望可以看看牠，看看是誰在跟我作對，哪怕只是瞄一眼也好。

老人根據星象判斷，這條魚整夜都沒有改變路線或方

向。太陽下山後，天氣就變冷了，汗水在老人的背脊、手臂和衰老的腿上早就乾了，他感覺到一點寒意。白天時，他把蓋在餌箱上的袋子攤在陽光下曬乾，太陽下山後，他就把這個袋子綁在脖子上，讓它垂在背上，再小心地把它墊在繞過肩膀的釣索下面。有袋子墊著釣索，他又想辦法傾身靠在船頭上，這樣子就可以算是很舒服了。其實這個姿勢不過是好過一點而已，但是他認為這樣可以算是很舒服了。

他心想，我拿牠沒有辦法，牠也拿我沒辦法。照這樣下去，對誰都沒有好處。

他一度站起來，在船邊撒尿，順便看看星象，確定航道。釣索在水中彷彿一道粼光，從他的肩膀直伸下去。他們現在移動得比較緩慢了，哈瓦那的燈光也變得比較黯淡，所以他知道潮流正帶著他們往東走。他心想，如果看不見哈瓦那的燈光，我們可能會更偏東方。假如這條魚的路線不變，我就還有好幾個小時可以看到燈光。不知道今天大聯盟棒球賽的結果怎麼樣，他心想。要是有一臺收音機就好了。他又想，我怎麼老是在想這個，應該多想想現在正在做的事情。你可不能做傻事啊。

於是他大聲說道：「如果那孩子在這裡就好了。他可以幫幫我，也可以見識到這個場面。」

人上了年紀，就不應該孤孤單單的。可是這是無法避免的事。我一定要記得在鮪魚腐壞之前吃一點，才能保持體

力。記住，不管你多麼沒胃口，你都得在早上吃掉。他對自己說，千萬要記住。

晚上，船邊來了兩隻鼠海豚，聽得見牠們在那兒翻滾、噴氣。他能夠分辨雄性的噴氣聲和雌性的嘆息聲。

「牠們好乖，」他說，「牠們嬉戲玩耍，彼此相親相愛。牠們和飛魚一樣，是我們的兄弟。」

然後，他開始同情他釣到的那隻大魚。牠很了不起，也很特別，不知道年齡有多大，他心想。我從來沒釣過這麼強壯，又這麼古怪的魚。也許牠太聰明了，才不肯跳起來。牠只要跳一下，或是猛衝一下，就會要了我的命。但也許牠以前上過幾次鉤，牠知道應該用這種方法對抗。牠不會知道，只有一個人在和他對抗，而且這個人只是個老頭子。可是，牠真是條大魚啊，如果送到市場上，肉還很新鮮的話，價錢一定很高。牠吃起餌來像隻公魚，拖著釣索也像隻公魚，而且戰鬥時毫不驚慌。不知道牠有什麼計畫？還是和我一樣無助？

他想起曾經釣到一對馬林魚中的一隻。雄魚總是讓雌魚先吃，因此上鉤的是條雌魚，牠驚惶狂暴，絕望地掙扎，很快就筋疲力竭，而那隻雄魚一直陪著牠，穿過釣索，在水面上繞著牠打轉。雄魚靠得很近，老人很擔心牠會用尾巴把釣索割斷，牠的尾巴和大鐮刀一樣鋒利，尺寸和形狀也和大鐮刀差不多。老人用魚叉刺雌魚，用棍子打牠，再握住牠那邊

緣像砂紙、形如長劍的尖喙,在牠的頭頂上猛敲,直到牠的顏色轉變得鏡子背面的顏色般了無生氣,才在男孩的協助下,把牠拖到船上,而雄魚依然在小船四周游動。老人在收拾釣索、安置魚叉時,雄魚竟然在船邊高高地跳到空中,想要看看雌魚在哪裡,然後潛入水中,牠那淡紫色的翅膀,也就是胸鰭,大大地伸展開來,身上一條條淡紫色的寬條紋全露了出來。老人記得,牠美麗極了,而且始終徘徊不去。

那是我在魚身上看過最悲哀的事情,老人心想。男孩也很難過,我們請求母魚的原諒,很快就把牠切割開來。

「真希望那孩子在這裡。」他大聲說著,靠在船頭的圓木板上,經由繞過肩膀的釣索感覺到大魚的力量,牠仍然穩穩朝著牠選定的方向前進。

老人心想,牠既然中了我的圈套,就得打定主意。

牠打的主意是潛在黝黑的深海裡,遠離所有的陷阱、圈套和詭計。而我的主意卻是搶在所有人之前找到牠。搶在世界上所有人之前。現在,我們已經在一塊兒,從中午一直到現在,雙方都沒有外力支援。

也許我不應該當漁夫,他心想。可是我天生就是幹這一行的。我一定要記得在天亮以後吃那條鮪魚。

天亮前不久,有什麼東西咬了他後面的一個餌。老人聽到樹枝折斷的聲音,釣索開始沿著船邊衝出去。在黑暗中,他從刀鞘抽出小刀,用左肩承受那條魚所有的牽引力,身體後仰,把釣索抵在船邊上割斷。他接著又割斷另一條靠近他的釣索,並摸黑把備用釣索的兩端打成結。他

只用一隻手就靈巧地解決了這件事,同時把腳放在釣索盤上,以便把結綁緊。現在他有六捲備用釣索了,每一個切斷的餌都有兩捲備用釣索,這條魚咬住的餌也有兩捲,這下子全都連在一起了。

他心想,天亮以後,我要回過頭去把剩下的那條四十噚的餌切斷,把那部分的備用釣索也連到這裡來。我會損失兩百噚高級的卡塔蘭釣索、釣鉤和鉤線。可是那些東西都可以替換。如果我釣上其他的魚,卻被那條大魚溜掉,誰能幫我替換大魚呢?

我不知道剛剛是什麼魚吃了那個餌,可能是條馬林魚,也可能是闊嘴鯊或其他的鯊魚。我根本來不及去判斷,我處置得太快了。

他大聲說道:「真希望那孩子在這裡。」

可是孩子並沒有和你在一起,他心想。你只能靠你自己,不管是不是在黑暗中,你最好現在就回過頭去處理最後那條線,把它割斷,再把備用釣索接起來。

他這麼做了。在黑暗中很難工作,那條魚還一度掀起大浪,使他面朝下撲倒,眼睛下方摔裂了一道傷口。他的臉頰流下一條血絲,但是凝結得很快,還沒有流到下巴就乾了。他勉強回到船頭,靠在船板上休息,並調整肩上的袋子,把釣索輕輕移到肩上另一個位置,繼續用肩膀撐著線,先小心地試探魚的拉力,再把一隻手伸到水中,感受小船的速度。

為什麼牠剛才會突然搖晃呢?他心想。一定是釣索在牠小丘般的背上滑動,但是牠的背絕不會比我的痠痛。可是,

牠總不能永遠拖著這條船，不論牠有多麼龐大。現在有可能造成麻煩的東西都清除掉了，而且我有一大捲備用釣索，再也沒有別的要求了。

「魚啊，」他的聲音很大，但是很溫柔。「我會一直陪著你，直到我死為止。」

我想牠也會一直陪著我，老人心裡想著，一邊等待黎明。現在還沒天亮，他感覺很冷，就緊貼著船板取暖。他想，只要牠做得到，我也可以。天際泛白時，釣索滑溜出去，直下海底。小船穩定地移動，在太陽露出一角時，陽光正好灑在老人的右肩上。

「牠在往北走。」老人說。潮水會把我們帶到遙遠的東方，他心想。真希望那條魚會順著潮水轉向，因為那表示牠累了。

太陽升得更高時，老人發現那隻魚一點都不累。只有一個好現象，就是從釣索的斜度可以知道，牠游的地方沒有那麼深了。這未必表示牠會跳躍，但還是有這個可能。

「老天爺，讓牠跳吧，」老人說。「我有夠長的釣索來對付牠。」

也許我把釣索拉緊一點，牠會覺得痛，因而跳了起來，他心想。現在天亮了，讓他跳吧，這樣一來，牠背脊骨旁邊的氣囊會充滿空氣，牠就不能潛到深海而死在那裡了。

他試圖拉緊釣索，可是自從他釣到那條魚以來，釣索就

緊繃得快要斷裂，他後仰著身體去拉，感覺到強勁的力道，知道釣索已經緊得不能再緊了。他心想，我不能用力去扯。每扯一下就把鉤子刺破的傷口拉大一些，等牠跳起來時，牠可能會把鉤子甩掉。不管怎樣，太陽讓我感覺好多了，至少這次我不用一直盯著它看。

釣索上纏著黃色的海草，但是老人知道那只會增加那條魚的負擔，所以他很高興。那是黃色的馬尾藻，就是它在前一天晚上發出許多粼光。

「魚啊，」他說，「我很愛你，也很敬佩你。可是我要在今天結束以前殺死你。」

但願是這樣，他想。

有隻小鳥從北方朝著小船飛過來。那是一隻刺嘴鶯，飛得離水面很近。老人看得出來牠非常疲倦。鳥兒飛到船尾，在那裡停歇。然後牠在老人的頭上繞了繞，在比較舒服的釣索上落腳。

「你多大了？」老人問那隻鳥。「這是你第一次飛行嗎？」

他說話時，鳥兒看著他。牠疲倦得無法去檢查那條釣索，細緻的腳爪緊緊抓著，在上面晃來晃去。

「釣索很穩當，」老人告訴牠。「太穩當了。昨天晚上沒有風，你不應該那麼累的，你們這些鳥兒是怎麼了？」

他想，那些老鷹出海就是為了捕捉這種小鳥。可是他沒有說出來，反正小鳥聽不懂他的話，而牠很快就會知道老鷹的厲害了。

「好好休息吧，小鳥兒，」他說，「然後跟人類、鳥兒或魚兒一樣，飛到陸地去碰碰運氣。」

他的背經過一夜已經僵硬了，現在痛得要命，於是他藉著說話提振精神。

「鳥兒啊，只要你願意，你可以在我家住下。」他說，「很抱歉，我不能趁著微風吹起時升起風帆載你回去，因為我正陪著一個朋友。」

就在這個時候，那條魚猛然翻動，把老人拖倒在船頭。如果他沒有坐穩，並及時放出一些釣索，可能就會被拉下船。

鳥兒在釣索突然被扯動時飛走了，老人並沒有注意到。他用右手輕撫釣索，發現手在流血。

「一定是什麼東西弄痛了牠。」他大聲說道，然後用力把釣索拉回，試試看是否能改變那條魚的方向。可是他把線

拉到即將繃裂時，就穩定姿勢，用身體後仰的力道來支撐釣索的拉力。

「魚啊，你現在感覺到痛了吧，」他說，「老天知道，我也是。」

他四處張望，找尋那隻鳥，想要找牠作伴，可是那隻鳥飛走了。

你並沒有停留多久，老人心想。可是你飛去的地方風浪較大，要到岸上才平安。我怎麼會讓那條魚猛一拉扯就把手劃破呢？我一定是太蠢了。可能是因為我把注意力都放在那隻小鳥身上，滿腦子想的都是牠。現在我要專心工作了，我也得吃點鮪魚，才能保持體力。

「真希望那孩子在這裡，也希望我有一些鹽。」他大聲說。

他把釣索的重量移到左肩，小心彎下膝蓋，在海裡洗洗手，然後把手放在水裡浸泡了一分多鐘，望著血絲順水漂去，還有小船移動時海水在他手上規律地搖晃。

「牠游得慢多了。」他說。

老人很想把手放在鹽水裡浸久一點，可是他擔心那條魚又會再度翻動，所以就站起來，穩住身體，把手舉向太陽。只是被釣索割傷了皮肉而已，可是那是他工作用的手。他知道在了結這件事之前，他都必須用到他的手，很不高興事情還沒有開始就掛了彩。

「現在，」他把手晾乾了以後說，「我得把那隻小鮪魚

吃下去。我可以用魚叉取來，在這裡舒舒服服地吃。」

　　他彎下膝蓋，用魚叉把船尾底下的鮪魚弄到自己身邊，小心不碰到成捲的釣索。他再度用左肩去拖釣索，以左手和手臂撐住，再從魚叉取下鮪魚，把魚叉放回原位。他一個膝蓋壓在魚身上，把魚從後頭部到尾巴縱切成深紅色的肉條，全是楔形的長條，沿著背脊骨一直切到肚子邊。切出六條肉塊之後，再把它們攤在船頭的木板上，然後在褲子上把刀子抹乾淨，拎起尾巴，把整個魚骨骸扔到大海裡。

　　「我大概吃不下一整條。」他說，用刀子橫切一條肉塊。他感覺到釣索沉穩的拉力，接著左手就抽筋了。他厭惡地瞪著那隻緊握著沉重釣索的手。

　　「這是怎麼樣的手啊，」他說。「你要抽筋就抽筋吧，把自己繃成一隻鳥爪，對你又沒有好處。」

　　來吧，他心想，順著釣索的斜度俯視黝黑的海水。吃吧，好讓那隻手有力氣。又不是那隻手的錯，你和這條魚已經鬥了好幾個小時了，但你可以和牠永遠鬥下去，現在把這條魚吃了吧。

　　他拿起一塊肉，放進嘴裡，慢慢咀嚼。味道並不壞。

　　他心想，多嚼幾下，把肉汁都吞進去。如果可以加一點萊姆汁、檸檬或鹽巴，應該會很不錯。

　　「手啊，你覺得怎麼樣？」他問那隻抽筋的手，它僵硬得像具死屍。「我會為你多吃一點。」

　　他把剛才切成兩半的另一部分也吃下去。他細細咀嚼，把魚皮吐掉。

「手啊，效果怎麼樣？現在要知道還太早嗎？」

他吃下另一整條魚肉，慢慢嚼著。

「這是隻健壯、血氣旺盛的魚，」他心想，「我運氣好捕到了牠，而不是隻海豚。海豚太甜了。這一隻一點都不甜，所有精力都還在裡面。」

不過講求實際才有意義，他想。如果有些鹽就好了。不知道太陽會把剩下的魚肉曬壞還是曬乾，最好全部吃下去，雖然我並不餓。那條魚游得很平靜，也很穩定。我要把肉都吃光，這樣子就做好準備了。

「手啊，你要忍耐，」他說，「我是為你吃的。」

但願我能餵餵那條魚，他心想。牠是我的兄弟。可是我必須殺死牠，而我要做到就得保持強壯。他仔細緩慢地吃下所有楔形肉條。

他挺直腰桿，在褲子上擦了擦手。

「現在，」他說，「手啊，你可以放開釣索了，在你停止作怪之前，我都只要用右肩去對付牠。」他用左腳踩在左手握住的沉重釣索上，身體後仰，以支撐壓在背上的拉力。

「老天幫個忙，叫手不要再抽筋了，」他說，「因為我不知道那條魚在打什麼主意。」

可是牠似乎很冷靜，按著牠的計畫在做，他心想。牠的計畫是什麼呢？我的又是什麼？我必須依照牠的計畫來調整，畢竟牠是那麼的龐大。如果牠跳起來，我就可以殺掉牠了。可是，如果牠一直留在底下，我也只好和牠耗下去。

　　他在褲子上揉搓抽筋的手，想要使手指活絡一下，可是手掌打不開。也許讓太陽曬一曬，它就會鬆開了，他心想。也許等到營養的生鮪魚肉消化以後，手才會打開。如果我得用到這隻手，不管付出什麼代價，我都要把它打開。可是現在我不想硬把它掰開，讓它自己打開，自然而然地恢復。畢竟我昨晚為了解開許多釣索，而過度使用它。

　　他放眼瞭望整片海域，得知自己是多麼的孤單。但是他可以看到深黑色海水中的七彩虹光、在眼前筆直拉著的釣索，還有平靜海面上的奇異波動。由於信風快來了，雲層逐漸堆積，他再往前望，看到一群野鴨在水面上飛掠而過，在空中畫出影子，消失之後又再度出現。他知道，沒有人在海上是孤獨的。

　　他想到有些人在小船上時，看不到陸地就會驚慌失措。在天氣會突然轉壞的月份，他們的擔心是對的。但現在是颶風季節，只要沒有颶風，那颶風季節的天氣就是整年中最好的。

　　如果有颶風要來，而你又在海上，你在幾天之前就會在天空看到徵兆了。他們在陸地上就看不到，因為他們不知道要怎麼看，他想。在陸地上應該也看得出有什麼不同，譬如雲層的形狀。不過現在不會有颶風要來。

　　他仰望天空，看到白色的積雲好像一層層可口的冰淇淋，而更高的捲雲則像稀疏的羽毛，襯托著九月的晴空。

　　「微風，」他說，「這種天氣對我比對你有利，魚兒。」

他的左手還在抽筋,不過他慢慢地把它伸展開來。

我最恨抽筋了,他想。這簡直就是身體的反叛。因食物中毒而在他人面前上吐下瀉是很丟臉的事,而抽筋就是丟自己的臉,尤其是單獨一人的時候。

如果那孩子在這裡,他就會幫我揉一揉,從前臂往下按摩,他想。不過它會自己放鬆的。

這時,還沒看到釣索在水中的斜度有改變,他的右手就感覺到拉力有些不同了。接著,就在他彎身去支撐釣索,左手用力在大腿上拍打時,他看到傾斜的釣索緩慢地往前升起。

「牠要上來了,」他說,「手啊,快點好起來,拜託好起來。」

釣索緩慢而穩定地上升,船頭的水面波濤洶湧,那條魚現身了。牠不停地冒上來,水從牠的兩旁傾瀉而下。在太陽下,牠是那麼的耀眼,牠的頭和背是深紫色的,兩側的寬紋在陽光下呈現淡紫。牠的尖嘴有一根棒球棍那麼長,尖得像一把劍。牠全身都浮上水面了,然後又輕巧地潛入水中,有如潛水伕。老人看到牠巨大的鐮刀狀尾巴沒入水中,釣索也跟著奔向前去。

「牠比這艘小船還長兩呎。」老人說。釣索飛快而穩定地滑出去,那條魚一點都不驚慌。老人在不使釣索扯斷的範圍內,用雙手極力握住釣索。他知道如果他用穩固的壓力把魚拉住,牠會拖走所有的釣索,並把它扯斷。

牠是條大魚,我一定要制服牠,他想。我絕不能讓牠知

道牠的力量有多大，也不能讓牠知道該怎麼逃跑。如果我是牠，我現在就會拚命地跑，直到把釣索扯斷為止。可是，謝謝老天爺，牠們不如我們這些殺手聰明，儘管牠們比我們更高貴，也更有能耐。

老人見過許多大魚，其中有很多都超過一千磅重，而他這輩子也曾捕獲兩條那麼重的，但是那時候他並不是單獨一人。現在他單獨一人，遠離陸地，和一條他從沒見過也從沒聽說過的最大的魚在一起，而他的左手仍然和繃緊的鷹爪一樣僵硬。

它會停止抽筋的，他心想。當然它要停止抽筋，才能去幫助右手。這裡有三樣東西是親兄弟：那條魚和我的兩隻手。抽筋一定要停止。手一抽筋就沒有用了。那條魚又再度慢下來，照著牠之前的速度前進。

不知道為什麼牠要跳起來，老人心想。他跳起來好像是為了向我顯示牠有多麼巨大。不管怎樣，我現在知道了，他想。真希望我可以讓牠知道我是個怎麼樣的人，可是那樣牠就會看到我抽筋的手了。讓牠把我想得比我本身還強健吧，到時候我也真會如牠所想地那樣強壯。他想，真希望我是那條魚，可以用所有的一切來對付我，而我只不過是有一點意志力和腦力罷了。

他舒服地靠在木板上，咬著牙承受不時發作的痛楚。那條魚穩定地游動，小船緩緩滑過黝黑的海水。從東方吹來的風掀起微波，到了中午，老人的手就不再抽筋了。

「魚啊，這對你是個壞消息，」他說，把釣索從披在肩膀上的麻袋移開。

雖然覺得很舒服，他卻一直感到疼痛，儘管他不願承認有疼痛這回事。

「我不是很虔誠，」他說，「可是只要能抓到這條魚，我願意唸十遍天主經和十遍聖母經。我也發誓，如果逮到牠，我就去柯布雷的聖母堂那裡朝聖。我發誓。」

他開始機械式地唸起禱告文。有時他疲倦得記不起經文，就快速地唸過去，讓經文自己跑出來。聖母經比天主經好唸多了，他想。

「萬福瑪利亞，妳充滿聖寵，主與妳同在，妳在婦女中受讚頌，妳的親子耶穌同受讚頌。天主聖母瑪利亞，求妳現在和我們臨終時，為我們罪人祈求天主。阿門。」他又加了一句：「萬福聖母，求您賜這條魚死，雖然牠很了不起。」

說完了祈禱文，他覺得好多了，可是疼痛並沒有減輕，也許還更劇烈了些。他倚靠在船頭的木板上，開始下意識地活動左手的指頭。

這時太陽已經很酷熱了，雖然有微風輕輕吹起。

「我最好還是把船尾那根細釣線重新裝上魚餌，」他說，「如果那條魚還要再堅持一個晚上，我就要再吃點東西，而且水瓶裡的水也剩下不多了。我想，這裡除了海豚什麼也釣不到，不過如果能趁新鮮時吃，海豚的味道並不差。希望今天晚上會有隻飛魚跳上船，可是我沒有燈光去引誘牠

們。飛魚生吃是再好不過的，而且不需要用刀子切。我現在必須盡量節省體力。天啊，我沒有料到牠是這麼的龐大。」

「可是，我會宰了牠的，」他說，「不管牠有多麼龐大，有多麼壯觀。」

這真是不公平，他想。可是，我要讓牠瞧瞧一個人能夠做到什麼、能夠承受什麼。

「我跟那孩子講過，我是個奇怪的老頭子，」他說，「現在是證明的時候了。」

以前證明過的一千次都不算什麼，現在他要再一次去求證。每一次都是新的開始，每次這麼做的時候，他都不會回顧過去。

希望牠睡著了，這樣我就可以睡一下，再去夢見獅子，他想。為什麼獅子是腦子裡留下來的最主要東西？不要想了，老頭子，他告訴自己。輕輕靠在木板上，什麼都不要想了。牠正在勞動，而你最好盡量減少勞動。

已經是下午了，小船依然緩慢穩定地移動。不過，來自東方的微風增加了一點阻力，老人隨著些微的波浪悠緩地前進，橫勒在背部的繩索變得沒有那麼痛了。

到了下午，釣索又開始上升。可是那條魚只是稍微往上移而已，仍然繼續游著。太陽照在老人的左臂、肩膀和背上，所以他知道那條魚已經轉向東北方了。

既然他曾和那條魚打過一次照面，他可以想像牠在水中游動的情形：牠那紫色的胸鰭像翅膀一樣伸展，筆直的大尾

巴在黑暗中滑過。不知道牠在那樣的深度可以看到多少東西，老人心想。牠的眼睛很大，馬的眼睛比牠小很多，但是可以在晚上看到東西。我以前在晚上也能看得很清楚，當然不是在漆黑的情況下，可是和貓的視力差不多。

因為太陽光和他不斷活動手指的關係，他左手完全不抽筋了。他開始把一些重量移到那裡，並且聳聳肩膀，活動背上的肌肉，以減輕繩索造成的疼痛。

「魚啊，如果你還不累，」他大聲說，「那你就太奇怪了。」

他現在覺得累極了，也知道快要入夜了，就盡量去想別的事情。他想到大聯盟，他都是用西班牙語來說這三個字，而他知道紐約的洋基隊正在和底特律的老虎隊比賽。

這已經是第二天我不知道比賽結果了，他想。可是我一定要有信心，我也不能輸給了不起的狄馬吉歐，雖然他的腳後跟長骨刺很痛，還是可以把什麼事情都做得很漂亮。什麼是骨刺？他問自己，並用西班牙語說了一遍「骨刺」。我們都沒長過。那會像被鬥雞的鐵刺插入腳後跟那麼痛嗎？我想我沒辦法忍受那種痛，也沒辦法像鬥雞那樣有一眼或兩眼瞎了還能繼續戰鬥。跟鳥獸比起來，人實在不算什麼。我還是寧願當那隻潛在深黑海水中的巨獸。

「但願鯊魚不會來，」他大聲說，「如果鯊魚來了，請老天爺可憐牠和我。」

　　你認為了不起的狄馬吉歐會像我陪這條魚一樣，陪一條魚這麼久嗎？他心想。我確定他會，而且比我更久，因為他年輕力壯。何況他的父親也是漁夫。可是骨刺會不會讓他痛得受不了？

　　「我不知道，」他大聲說，「我從來沒有長過骨刺。」

　　太陽下山時，為了增強信心，他回想起有一次在卡薩布蘭加的酒館，和一個從聖菲哥斯來的，全碼頭最強壯的黑人巨漢比腕力的情形。足足有一天一夜，他們兩人把胳膊放在畫了粉筆線的桌子上，手臂直立，拳頭握得緊緊的。雙方都卯足了勁，想把對方的手壓倒在桌上。下賭注的人很多，觀眾在煤油燈照亮的房間裡進進出出，而他直盯著黑人的胳膊、手和臉。最初的八個小時過後，他們每四個小時就換一個裁判，好讓裁判輪流睡覺。血從他和黑人的指甲底下滲出來，他們瞪著彼此的眼睛、手和前臂，打賭的人在房間裡來來去去，坐在牆邊的高腳椅上觀看。牆壁是用木板釘的，漆成亮藍色，燈光把他們的

影子打在上面。黑人的影子很巨大，在牆上隨著被微風撼動的燈火不時地晃動。

他們整晚纏鬥，你來我往。人們給黑人灌萊姆酒，為他點菸。

灌下萊姆酒後，黑人力氣倍增，一度把老人的手臂壓下三吋。當時老人還不老，他是桑地亞哥選手。不過，老人又把手扳回原位。那時他就有把握打敗黑人，雖然他是個好人，也是一等一的好手。天亮時，打賭的人要求宣佈平手，裁判也頻頻搖頭，老人卻使盡力氣，把黑人的手一點一點地往下壓，終於壓倒在桌上。

比賽是從星期天早上開始的，結束時已經是星期一早上了。許多打賭的人要求和局，因為他們得去碼頭搬糖包，或是去哈瓦那煤礦公司幹活。不然的話，每個人都很想看到他們分出勝負。但不管怎樣，他都在大家要去上工前做了個了斷。

那件事過後很長一段時間，大家都叫他「冠軍」，第二年春天他們又比了一次。但是這回賭金不大，而且他兩三下就把賭金贏到手了，因為之前的比賽已經使聖菲哥斯的黑人失去了信心。在那之後，老人又和人比了幾次，然後就不再比了。他深信只要他想贏，就能夠擊敗任何人，但是比賽會傷了他用來捕魚的右手。他練習過幾次用左手比腕力，可是他的左手總是像個叛徒，不願依他的指令做事，他也就無法信任它。

　　太陽應該把手烘熱了，他想。它不該再抽筋了，除非晚上的氣溫降得太低。不知道今晚會發生什麼事。

　　一架飛機掠過他的頭頂，往邁阿密飛去。他望著飛機的影子把成群的飛魚嚇得驚跳起來。

　　「飛魚這麼多，這裡一定有海豚。」他說，身體往後仰，看看是否能拉回一點釣索。可是沒有辦法，釣索仍然繃得很緊，水珠在上面抖動，好像快要斷掉了。小船緩慢地前行，他一直望著飛機，直到它離開視線為止。

　　在飛機裡面的感覺一定很怪，他想。從那麼高的地方往下看，不知道海洋是什麼樣子？如果飛得不太高，他們應該看得到那條魚。我真希望能夠飛在兩百噚的高空，從上面看那條魚。以前在捕龜船上，我曾待在桅杆頂端的橫桁上，即使是那樣的高度，視野都會變得很廣闊。在那裡，海豚的顏色看起來更綠，還看得到牠們的條紋和紫色斑點，以及牠們一整群的游動。為什麼能在深暗的水流中快速游動的魚類都有紫色的背部，而且通常都有紫色條紋或斑點？當然海豚看起來是綠色的，因為牠們實際上是金色的。可是在牠餓了想吃東西時，紫色條紋就會在側邊顯現，就跟馬林魚一樣。那是因為憤怒，或是速度較快，才產生那些條紋的嗎？

　　快要天黑時，他們經過一大叢馬尾藻，那些海藻在輕波中浮動搖晃，好像海洋正在一條黃色毛氈下和什麼東西做愛。細釣線釣到了一隻海豚。老人頭一眼看到牠時，牠正跳到空中，在夕陽餘暉下呈現金黃色，猛烈地扭動、撲擊。牠

在恐懼中一跳再跳，彷彿在表演特技。老人設法走到船尾，蹲下來用右手握住粗釣索，左手把海豚拖上船，同時用赤裸的左腳踩住每次拉上來的釣線。魚上了船尾，死命地跳來跳去。老人靠到船尾，把這條帶著紫斑、金光閃閃的魚提起來。牠銜著魚鉤的下顎不斷地張合，用牠扁長的身體，連同頭和尾拍打著船板，老人用木棍朝牠閃亮的金色頭顱敲下去，牠一陣痙攣，就不再動了。

　　老人從魚頭解下鉤子，用另一條沙丁魚重新裝上餌，再把釣線拋進海裡。然後他慢慢走回船頭，洗了洗他的左手，在褲子上擦一擦，把沉重的釣索從右手移到左手，再把右手伸到水裡洗，同時望著沉入海中的太陽，以及那條傾斜的粗釣索。

「牠一點都沒有變。」他說。但是看著手邊翻滾的水花時，他發現魚的速度明顯減慢了。

「我來把兩隻槳橫綁在船尾上，好讓牠在晚上放慢速度。」他說，「他在晚上精力充沛，我也一樣。」

等一會兒再剖開海豚比較好，這樣才能保留肉裡面的血，他想。我可以晚一點再弄，那時候再把槳綁起來，好拖慢速度。我現在最好讓那條魚安靜，不要在日落時干擾牠。所有的魚在日落的時候都不好對付。

他把手舉起來風乾，然後用那隻手抓住釣索，盡可能讓自己舒服一點，往前靠在船板上，讓魚拉著走，這樣船承載的重量就會跟他一樣，或者比他還多。

我漸漸知道怎麼對付牠了，他想。至少這個方式還過得去。何況，牠自從吞了那個餌以後就沒有吃過東西，而牠是那麼龐大，需要很多食物。我已經吃下一整隻鮪魚了，明天我可以吃海豚。他用西班牙語說「海豚」。也許我應該在切洗牠時吃一點。海豚比鮪魚難吃，不過話說回來，沒有什麼事是簡單的。

「魚啊，你覺得怎樣？」他大聲問道。「我覺得很好，而且我的左手好多了，我又有一天一夜的食物可以吃。魚啊，繼續拖船吧。」

他並沒有真的覺得很好，因為勒在背後的繩索已經痛得幾乎超出能忍受的極限，已經令他麻木得無法確信。可是我遇到過更糟的情況，他心想。我的手只是稍微割傷而已，而

且另一隻手也不再抽筋了。我兩隻腳都沒事，在糧食的補給上，我也比牠強。

這時天黑了，因為在九月，太陽一下山，天馬上就暗下來。他躺臥在腐朽的船頭板上，盡可能地休息。第一批星星出現了，有一顆星叫做利格星，他不知道這個名字，但是看到它就知道其他星星很快就會出現，他就會有許多遙遠的朋友作伴。

「那條魚也是我的朋友，」他大聲說。「我從來沒有看過，也沒有聽說過這種魚，可是我一定要殺死牠。很高興我們用不著想辦法殺死星星。」

想想看，如果人每天都必須想辦法殺死月亮，那有多糟，他想著。月亮會逃走的。再想想看，如果人每天都必須去殺太陽，那又會怎麼樣？因此，我們還是很幸運的，他想。

然後，他開始可憐那條大魚，牠沒有東西吃，然而他的同情心並沒有減損想要殺死大魚的決心。他想，牠的肉不曉得可以供多少人吃。可是，那些人有資格吃牠嗎？沒有，當然沒有。從牠高尚的舉止和威嚴來看，沒有人夠資格吃牠。

我實在不懂得這些事情，他想。但我們不必想辦法去殺死太陽或月亮或星星，真是太好了。光是在海上討生活，殺死我們的親兄弟就夠我們受的了。

現在，我必須想想該怎麼增加阻力。這有好處也有壞處。如果綁好的船槳產生阻力，船身變重，而牠又盡全力去

拖，我可能就要放出很多釣索，到最後會讓牠給溜了。但是船身太輕又會延長我們雙方的痛苦，不過這方面對我比較安全，畢竟牠還沒有發揮最快的速度。不管怎樣，我都得剖開這隻海豚，免得牠腐壞了。我也要吃一點，好維持體力。

現在，我要休息一個多小時，等到覺得牠穩定下來了，我再去船尾幹活，再決定怎麼辦。在這同時，我可以注意牠的舉動，看看有什麼變化。船槳是個好主意，可是這個時候安全比較重要！畢竟那是隻了不起的魚，我看到鉤子卡在牠的嘴角，牠的嘴卻閉得緊緊的。鉤子的痛苦並不算什麼。飢餓的痛苦，還有必須對抗某個牠不明瞭的東西才難受呢。老頭子，先歇一歇吧，讓牠去勞動，等輪到你動手時再說。

他估計自己休息了兩個小時。月亮遲遲沒有升起，使他無法判斷時間。他並沒有真的睡著，只是比較放鬆而已。他的肩膀上仍然擔負著那條魚的拉力，不過他把左手放在船頭舷上，逐漸把拉力移到船身。

如果釣索可以固定，事情就簡單了。可是只要輕輕一扯，牠就會把釣索扯斷。我必須用身體去緩和釣索的拉力，並隨時準備好用雙手放線。

「可是你還沒有睡覺呢，老頭子，」他大聲說。「已經過了半個白天和一整夜，現在又是另外一天了，你都沒有睡覺。你必須想辦法睡一下，趁牠安靜穩定的時候。如果你不睡，你的腦袋可能會變得不清楚。」

我的腦筋很清楚，他想。太清楚了，跟星星一樣清楚，它們是我的兄弟。但是我還是得睡一下。星星要睡覺，太陽

和月亮要睡覺，連海洋在平靜無波的時候也會睡個幾天。

記得要睡覺，他想。你要想個簡單妥當的辦法安置釣索，然後強迫自己去睡。現在先回船尾處理那條海豚。如果你要睡覺，就不能用船槳去製造阻力，那太危險了。

我不睡覺也撐得下去，他對自己說。可是那樣子太危險了。

他開始用手和膝蓋爬到船尾，以免驚動那條魚。牠可能正半睡半醒著，他想。可是我不要讓牠休息。牠必須拖船，拖到死為止。

回到船尾後，他轉過身來，用左手握住從肩膀繞過來的釣索，再用右手拔出刀鞘裡的小刀。現在星星很明亮，可以清楚地看見海豚。他用刀刃刺進牠的頭，把牠從船尾底下拖過來，然後一腳踩在海豚身上，俐落地從牠的切到下頷邊緣，接著放下刀子，用右手掏出內臟，清理內部，除去魚鰓。

他的手感覺到海豚的胃部沉沉滑滑的，他把它剖開，裡面有兩隻飛魚，又新鮮又緊緻。他把飛魚並排擺著，再把內臟和魚鰓從船尾丟出去。那堆東西下沉時，在水裡劃出一道粼光。海豚在星光下顯得冰冷，呈現醜陋的灰白色。老人仍然用右腳踩住牠的頭，先剝下一邊的皮，再把它翻過來剝另一邊的皮，接著從頭到尾剖下兩邊的肉。

他把殘骸扔出船外，看水中有沒有出現漩渦，可是那裡只有東西緩慢下沉的光影。他轉過身來，把兩隻飛魚塞在兩片海豚肉裡面，刀子收進刀鞘，然後慢慢將身子移到船頭。

他的背脊因為釣索的重量而彎曲，海豚肉是用右手捧著。

回到船頭，他把兩片海豚肉放在木板上，旁邊擱著飛魚。接著他把肩膀上的釣索調整到另一個位置，再度用擱在船舷的左手握住。然後他在船邊彎下身子，在水裡清洗飛魚，同時留意海水在手上滑移的速度。他的手因為剝了魚皮而發出燐光，但他仍盯著在上面游動的水流。水流減弱了。他把手伸到船板上搓揉時，水面上浮現點點燐光，緩緩漂到船尾。

「牠不是累了就是在休息，」老人說，「現在我趕快把海豚吃一吃，再休息一下，睡個覺。」

星光下的夜晚變得更冷了。他吃下半片海豚肉，還有一隻掏空腸肚、頭部切除的飛魚。

「海豚肉如果煮熟了，味道會很鮮美，」他說。「生吃實在是太難下嚥了。我以後出海一定要帶點鹽或萊姆。」

我如果夠聰明，就會在白天把水潑到船頭，等水乾了，就會產生一點鹽，他想。可是釣到海豚時，已經差不多是黃昏。不管怎麼說，我的準備都做得不夠。但是我把它全細細咀嚼後吃下去了，沒有噁心作嘔。

東邊的天空越來越陰沉，他熟知的星星也一一消失。船看起來似乎要航向一個雲彩的大峽谷，風速也減弱了。

「再過三、四天，天氣就要變壞了，」他說，「但是不會是今晚或明天。老頭子，現在你準備好可以睡覺了，趁這條魚安靜穩定的時候。」

他用右手緊緊抓住釣索，大腿抵著右手，把全身的重量都壓在船頭板上。然後他把肩膀上的釣索拉低一點，再用左手握住釣索。

只要有支撐，右手就會握住釣索。如果右手在我睡著時放鬆，我的左手會在釣索滑走時叫醒我。右手的負擔實在太重了，可是它已經很習慣吃苦。我就算只睡二十分鐘或半個小時，也會有好處。他的身體往前傾，用全身抵住釣索，把所有重量都壓在右手上，然後睡著了。

他沒有夢見獅子，而是夢見一大群海豚，分散的範圍有八或十哩那麼廣。由於正逢交配的季節，牠們會高高地跳到半空中，再落下來回到牠們跳起時形成的水渦中。

接著他夢到村莊，他躺在自己的床上，北風刮著，他覺得很冷。他的右臂也沉睡了，因為他的頭用它來代替枕頭。

接下來，他夢見長長的黃色沙灘，看到獅群中的第一隻在黃昏的昏暝中現身，然後其他獅子也來了，當時他的下巴是靠在船頭板上。他乘的船在岸邊停泊，黃昏的微風吹著，他等著看會不會有更多獅子過來，覺得好快樂。

月亮已經出來很久了，可是他繼續沉睡，那條魚也平穩地拉著，小船一路航向雲層的隧道裡。

他驚醒過來，因為他的右拳猛地朝他的臉撞去，釣索飛快滑過，使他的右手感到燒痛。他的左手已經麻木了，於是他用右手拚命控制，但是釣索還是不停的竄出。他的左手好不容易抓到了釣索，他仰著身子把釣索朝後拉，現在背上和

左手也有了燒痛的感覺。他的左手承受著所有重量，因此嚴重割傷了。他回頭去看備用的捲軸，釣索放得很順暢。就在這時候，那條魚跳了起來，產生巨大的波濤，然後重重落入海裡。牠一次又一次的跳躍，船的速度很快，儘管釣索仍在竄出，老人把釣索扯得都快斷了，一次又一次地扯到快要斷裂。他已經被拖倒，身體緊貼著船頭，整張臉埋在海豚肉片上，動也不能動。

　　他想，這就是我們所期待的，現在我們就來承擔吧。

　　我要讓牠賠償釣索，他想。一定要讓牠付出代價。

　　他看不到那條魚的跳躍，只聽得到海水飛濺和牠摔落時的轟然水聲。釣索的奔竄把他的手割得傷痕累累，可是這早

在他的意料之中,他只能設法讓釣索勒在長繭的地方,不讓釣索滑過手掌或是傷到手指。

如果那孩子在這裡,他就會用水弄溼那些線軸,他想。沒錯,那孩子在這裡就好了,那孩子在這裡就好了。

釣索不停不停地滑走,不過現在慢下來了,老人使那條魚每拖走一吋都要付出代價。這時他可以從船板上抬起頭來,海豚肉片已被他的臉頰壓碎。他先是彎下膝蓋,然後緩慢地站起身。他仍然在放出釣索,但是速度慢了很多。他努力後退,用腳去碰觸他看不到的捲軸。釣索還有很多,現在那條魚必須在水裡把這些釣索都拉走。

太好了,他心想。而且牠已經跳了十幾次了,背脊兩邊的浮袋充滿了空氣,所以牠不會沉得太深,不會死在我無法把牠拉上來的地方。牠很快就會開始兜圈子,到時候我一定要想出辦法來對付牠。不知道是什麼使牠突然激動起來?牠是因為飢餓才那麼拚命掙扎,還是因為在黑暗中有什麼東西嚇著牠了?也許牠是突然害怕起來。可是這條魚是那麼的鎮定、強壯,好像什麼都不怕,而且信心滿滿的。好奇怪啊。

「你最好不要害怕,相信自己,老頭子,」他說,「你現在又穩住牠了,可是你沒辦法把釣索收回來。不過,牠很快就會兜圈子了。」

老人用左手和肩膀來支撐那條魚,彎下身,用右手掬起一把海水,把臉上的碎海豚肉洗掉。他很擔心海豚肉會令他反胃,萬一嘔吐,就會傷了元氣。臉洗乾淨以後,他

把右手伸到船邊沖一沖，然後泡在鹽水裡，望著日出前出現的第一道曙光。牠正在朝東邊游去，他想。這表示牠累了，只好順著海潮走。牠很快就要兜圈子了，接著就要看我們的真工夫了。

他判斷右手在水裡泡得夠久了，於是把手伸出來瞧一瞧。「不嚴重，」他說，「疼痛對一個男人來說並不算什麼。」

他小心握住釣索，以免碰到剛割傷的地方，然後轉移那條魚的重量，好把左手從船的另一邊放進水裡。

「你這個廢物倒幹得不錯，」他對左手說，「可是之前有一陣子我都看不出你的能耐。」

我為什麼不是生下來就有兩隻好手呢？他想。或許是我自己的過錯，我沒有好好鍛鍊這一隻手。可是老天知道，它也曾經有足夠的學習機會。不過，它昨晚表現得還不算太差，只抽筋一次。如果它再抽筋，就讓釣索把它給切斷好了。

他想到這裡，就知道自己的腦筋不太清楚，覺得應該再吃一點海豚。可是，我做不到，他告訴自己。寧可頭暈，也不要因為嘔吐而傷了元氣。我知道就算我吃得下去，也沒辦法不吐，因為我的臉剛剛才貼在那裡。我把肉留下來以備萬一好了，直到它腐爛。想要靠營養來增加體力，現在哪來得及。你這個笨蛋，吃另一隻飛魚呀，他自言自語。

那隻飛魚就在那裡，乾乾淨淨的，隨時可以享用。他

用左手拿起魚，放進嘴中，仔細咀嚼魚骨，從頭到尾都下了肚子。

飛魚比任何一種魚都營養，他想。至少能提供我所需要的體力。現在我能做的都做了，他心想。讓那條魚開始兜圈子，開始這場搏鬥吧。

自從他出海以來，這是太陽第三度升起，那條魚開始兜圈子了。

從釣索的斜度並不能看出那條魚是否在兜圈子。要看出來還太早。老人只感覺得到釣索的拉力減少了一些，於是他開始輕輕用右手拉釣索。和之前一樣，釣索又扯緊了，可是緊到快要斷裂的的時候，它又變鬆了。他的肩膀和頭從釣索下面鑽出來，開始平穩輕緩地收回釣索。他的兩手左右晃動，用上身體和雙腳的全部力量，盡可能大把大把的拉。他的老腿和肩膀成為控制動作的支點。

「可真是個大圈子，」他說，「牠確實在轉圈了。」

不久釣索就再也收不進來了，老人緊緊握著它，直到看見水珠在陽光下從線上崩落。突然釣索猛滑出去，老人跪了下來，很不甘願地看著釣索溜進黑茫茫的水裡。

「牠正繞到圈子最遠的地方。」他說。我一定要盡量拉緊，他想。拉緊了，牠兜的圈子就會一次比一次小，也許一個小時內我就能看到牠了。現在我一定要馴服牠，然後把牠殺死。

可是兩個小時過後，那條魚仍然在慢慢轉著圈子，而老人渾身是汗，全身筋骨都感到疲累。不過圓圈已經小了很多，從釣索的斜度看來，可以知道那條魚正在一邊游一邊往上移動。

老人的眼前冒出黑點已經有一個小時了，鹹鹹的汗水刺痛了他的眼睛，也刺痛了眼眶和額頭上的傷口。他並不擔心黑點，因為這麼用力拉扯釣索，會出現黑點是很正常的。他已經有兩度覺得頭昏眼花，這才是他所在意的。

「我不能敗在這裡，死在一條魚手上，」他說，「現在我已經很漂亮地把牠弄到手，老天保佑我撐下去。我願意念一百次天主經和一百次聖母經，只是現在沒辦法念。」

就當作已經念過好了，他心想。我以後會補念的。

就在這時候，雙手握住的釣索突然晃動，力道又猛又重。

牠正在用尖喙撞擊金屬鉤線，他想。那是一定會發生的。牠非這麼做不可。可是那會使牠跳起來，我寧可牠繼續轉圈子。牠必須跳起來呼吸空氣，可是每跳一次就會把鉤傷的地方扯得更大，最後可能會甩掉鉤子。

「魚啊，別跳，」他說，「別跳！」

那條魚又撞了幾次金屬線，每次牠甩頭，老人就放出一點釣索。

我不能增加牠的痛苦，他想。我的痛苦沒有關係，我受得了，可是牠的痛苦會令牠發瘋的。

　　過了一會兒，那條魚停止碰撞金屬線，又開始慢慢兜圈子。老人現在可以穩穩收回釣索，可是他又頭暈了。他用左手掬起一把海水，淋在頭上，然後再取了一些揉搓頸背。

　　「我沒有抽筋，」他說，「牠很快就要冒出水面了，我撐得住的。你一定要撐到最後。」

　　他靠在船頭上跪下，暫時又把釣索勒在背上。我要趁著牠遠在那裡繞圈子時休息一會兒，等牠繞回來，我就要站起來對付牠。他打定了主意。

　　在船頭休息真是舒服，令他真想繼續讓那條魚自己去轉圈子，而不去收釣索。可是在釣索的張力顯示出那條魚就要轉向船身時，老人站起來，開始左右搖晃，把所有能夠收回的釣索收回來。

　　我從來沒有這麼疲倦過，他想，而現在信風吹起來了，正好可以趁這個時候把牠拖上來。我太需要那陣風了。

　　「牠下次游到遠處的時候我再休息，」他說，「我覺得好多了，等牠再轉個兩、三圈，我就要逮住牠。」

　　他的草帽已經掉到腦後，他在船頭坐下，藉著釣索的拉力感覺到魚在轉彎。

　　魚啊，你現在盡量活動，等你轉回來，我就要收拾你了。

　　海面起了相當多的浪，不過那是好天氣的風，他必須利用這陣風回家。

老人與海

「我只要划向西南方就好了，」他說，「人不會在海上迷失的，何況那是個長長的島。」

那條魚在繞第三圈時，他頭一次把牠看清楚了。

起初是一個黑影，過了很久才從船下穿行而過，軀體長得令他無法相信。

「不，」他說，「牠不可能那麼大！」

可是牠就是那麼大。兜完這一圈時，牠在距離老人只有三十碼的水面上現身，老人看到牠從水中露出來的尾巴，比一把大鐮刀的刀刃還大，在深藍色的水面上呈現淡淡的紫色。尾巴往後傾，魚就在水面下游著，老人看得到牠龐大的身軀和圍在身上的紫色條紋。牠的背鰭下垂，碩大的胸鰭往外伸展。

大魚在兜圈子時，老人看到牠的眼睛，牠身邊有兩隻灰色的印魚，有時緊靠著牠，有時離牠而去，有時又自在地在牠的影子中游動。那兩條魚都有三呎多長，游得很快時，全身會像鰻魚一般扭擺。

老人一直在冒汗，但不只是太陽的關係。那條魚每穩定地繞一圈，他就收回一些釣索。他確定牠再繞兩圈，他就有機會把魚叉刺進牠的體內。

可是，我得讓牠游過來一點，再過來，再過來，他想。我不能刺牠的頭，我得刺進牠的心臟。

「你要沉著，要堅強，老頭子。」他說。

　　繞下一圈時，魚背露了出來，可是離小船有點遠。而再下一圈時，牠還是離得太遠，不過在水面上浮得更高了，老人確定只要再收回一點釣索，就可以把牠拖到船邊。

　　他早就把魚叉準備好了，一綑連著魚叉的細繩放在圓形的籃子裡，一端牢牢繫在船頭的纜柱上。

　　現在魚又轉回來了，姿態平靜優美，只有碩大的尾巴在擺動。老人用盡全力把牠拉過來。剎那之間，魚側翻了一下，然後挺直身體，開始繞另一個圈子。

　　「我拖動牠了，」老人說，「我剛才拖動牠了。」

　　他又覺得頭暈了，但還是使盡力氣去拉住那條大魚。我拖動牠了，他心想。也許這一次我就能夠把牠弄過來。拉呀，手啊，老人想。站穩啊，腳兒。為我撐下去吧，頭呀，為我撐到最後，你從來沒有昏倒過。這回我一定要把牠拉過來。

　　可是老人集中力氣，在魚游到船邊之前就開始拚命地拉，那條魚卻傾向一邊，然後挺直身體，又游開了。

　　「魚啊，」老人說，「魚啊，反正你死定了，難道你也要把我整死？」

　　你這樣做是沒有用的，他想。他的嘴已經乾得說不出話來，但是他現在沒辦法伸手去拿水。我這次一定要把牠拖到船邊，他想。如果牠再多繞幾圈，我可能會撐不下去。不，沒這回事，他對自己說。你永遠都撐得下去。

　　在兜下一圈時，他差一點就把牠拉過來。可是這條魚再度挺直身體，慢慢游開。

　　魚啊，你整死我了，老人心想。可是你有權利這麼做。兄弟，我從來沒有見過比你更龐大，或是更美麗、更沉著、更高貴的東西。來殺我吧。我不在乎誰殺死誰了。

　　現在你的腦筋有點糊塗了，老頭子。你的頭腦一定要保持清醒。保持清醒，像個男人，或是跟這條魚一樣，懂得去忍受痛苦，他心想。

　　「腦袋，醒一醒，」他用幾乎聽不見的聲音說。「醒一醒。」

　　牠又轉了兩圈。

　　我真搞不懂，老人想。他每次都覺得自己要昏過去了。我真搞不懂，可是我要再試一次。

　　他又試了一次，覺得自己在翻動大魚時就要昏過去了。那條魚挺直身體，再度緩慢地游開，巨大的尾巴在空中搖擺。

　　我要再試一次，老人發誓，雖然他的手現在已經軟弱無力，視線也只有瞬間看得清晰。

　　他又試了一次，結果還是一樣。他於是心想，我要再試一次，而他還沒有開始用力，就又覺得快要暈倒了。我要再試一次。

　　他忍受所有的痛苦，使出僅存的力氣和消失許久的驕傲，去對抗那條魚臨死的痛苦。魚終於來到船邊，在他身邊

緩慢地游著，尖喙幾乎觸到了船板。牠開始經過船身，身軀很長很深、很寬，閃著銀光，上面圍繞著紫色的條紋，在水中無限地伸展開來。

老人丟下釣索，用腳踩住，然後盡量高舉魚叉，使出全力和剛才所振起的力量，插進魚的側身，就在那巨大胸鰭的後面，那片胸鰭高高地伸到空中，有老人的胸膛那麼高。

他感覺到鐵叉刺進去了，然後他靠過去，用全身的重量把叉子更往裡面推。

那條魚帶著致命的重創，突然恢復生氣，從水面高高躍起，展露牠雄偉的長度和寬度，還有牠的力量和美麗。牠似乎懸在老人與船的上空，然後轟隆一聲墜落水中，濺得老人和整艘小船都是水。

老人覺得頭暈很不舒服，而且視線模糊。但是他還是解開魚叉上的釣索，使釣索從他皮開肉綻的手慢慢滑出去，等到視線恢復時，他看到那條魚翻出白色的肚皮仰面躺著，魚叉柄斜插在魚的肩膀上，從牠的心臟噴出來的血液染紅

了海水。在深度超過一英哩的藍色海域中，深黑的血水起先好像聚集的魚群，然後像一片雲一樣擴散開來。魚泛著銀光，一動也不動地隨著浪潮浮沉。

老人仔細地檢視他眼前的景象，然後把魚叉的細繩在船頭的纜柱上繞了兩圈，才把頭埋進雙手間。

「頭腦要保持清楚，」他靠在船頭板上說。「我是個疲倦的老頭子，可是我已經殺了這條魚，牠是我的兄弟，現在我該去做苦差事了。」

我得準備套索和繩子來把牠綁在船邊，他想。即使只有我和牠兩個，如果把牠拖上船，船也會浸滿水，而就算把水舀出，這艘船也裝不下牠。我必須把東西都準備好，把牠拖過來綁好，然後豎好桅桿，張起帆回家。

他開始把魚拖到船邊，這樣子他才能把釣索穿進魚鰓，從魚嘴裡拉出來，將魚頭牢牢繫在船頭上。我想看看牠，他心想，我想摸摸牠，確定牠的存在。牠是我的財產，他想。可是這不是我想摸摸牠的原因。我想我摸到牠的心臟了，他想著，就在我第二次把魚叉柄推進去的時候。現在把牠拖過來綁好，分別用套繩套住牠的尾巴和身體中央，綁在船尾上吧。

「該幹活了，老頭子，」他說。他喝了一小口水。「戰鬥結束了，現在有非常多苦差事要做。」

他仰望天空，再看看他的魚，仔細端詳太陽。正午剛過

不久，他想。信風正在吹著。現在釣索已經用不著了，回家以後，我大可以和那孩子再把釣索接起來。

「魚啊，過來吧。」他說。可是魚沒有過來，牠只是躺在海裡，隨著波浪翻滾，老人只好把小船挪到牠那裡去。

他來到魚的身邊，把魚頭拴在船頭上時，仍然不敢相信牠有這麼龐大。但是他從纜柱解下魚叉繩，把它穿過魚鰓，從下顎抽出來，在尖嘴上繞了一圈，再把繩子穿進另一邊的鰓，又在尖嘴上繞了一圈，然後把兩股繩子連起來打個結，緊緊綁在船頭的纜柱上。他接著把繩子割下來，去船尾用繩子套住魚尾。魚已經由原來的紫色和銀色變成完全的銀色，牠的條紋顯出和尾巴一樣的淡紫色，寬度比一個人伸開了五指的手還寬。魚的眼睛看起來好像潛望鏡的鏡面或遊行儀式中的聖徒一般冷漠。

「只有這個方法可以殺死牠。」老人說。他喝了點水，感覺好多了。他知道他不會再頭暈了，而且頭腦很清楚。照魚的樣子看來，牠超過一千五百磅，他心想。也許更重。如果淨肉有三分之二的重量，照一磅三十分錢計算，該是多少呢？

「我需要用鉛筆來算，」他說，「我的頭腦沒有那麼清楚。可是我想今天連了不起的狄瑪吉歐也會為我感到驕傲。我沒有長骨刺，可是手和背真是痛得厲害。」不知道骨刺是什麼，他想著。也許我們有，只是不知道而已。

他把魚綁在船頭、船尾和中間的坐板上。這條魚這麼龐大，好像在船邊繫著一艘更大的船。他割下一段繩子，把魚的下顎和尖喙綁起來，這樣子牠的嘴就不會張開，他們就可以毫無阻礙地航行。他接著豎起桅桿，用魚鉤的桿子和將就使用的下桁，拉起滿是補丁的帆，船開始移動，他半躺在船尾，朝西南方航行。

他不需要指南針來告訴他西南方是哪裡。他只需要感覺到信風和帆的飄動就行了。我最好放一條繫著匙鉤的細釣線到海裡，設法弄點東西來吃，同時潤潤喉嚨。可是他找不到匙鉤，沙丁魚也都腐爛了。所以在船經過時，他用魚鉤撈起一些馬尾藻，用力搖晃，使裡面的小蝦跌到船板上。總共有十多隻小蝦，活蹦亂跳的，好像沙蚤。老人用姆指和食指招去蝦頭，放進嘴裡，連殼帶尾一起咀嚼。雖然蝦子很少，可是他知道蝦子很營養，味道也不錯。

老人的水瓶裡還有兩口水，吃完了蝦子，他喝了半口水。小船雖然負載沉重，卻航行得很順利。他駕船時，把舵柄夾在腋窩裡。他看得到那條魚，而且只要瞧瞧他的手，感覺到背靠在船尾上，他就知道這一切確確實實發生過，而不是一場夢。在事情快要結束時，他一度難受得要命，以為那可能是一場夢。然後他看到了那條魚躍上水面，在下墜之前懸在空中動也不動時，他很確定那是個奇蹟，不可思議得令他難以相信。當時他的視線很模糊，不過現在他可以看得跟以前一樣清楚了。

　　此時他知道魚就在那裡，雙手和背部的傷痛也都不是夢。手傷很快就會復原了，他心想。已經不流血了，鹽水會把傷口治好。這個海灣的深黑色海水是最好的藥。我唯一要做的就是保持頭腦清醒。兩隻手已經做好該做的工作，我們的航行也很順利。魚的嘴巴閉起，尾巴挺直，我們像兄弟一樣乘船回家。然後他的腦筋開始有點不清楚，他想著，是牠在帶著我走，還是我帶著牠走呢？如果我把牠拖在後頭，那就沒什麼疑問了。如果那條魚失去了所有尊嚴，被我載在船上，那也不會有任何疑問。可是我們是綁在一起航行，老人心想，就算是牠帶著我走吧，只要能讓牠高興。我只是懂得一些詭計才能勝過牠，而牠對我一點惡意都沒有。

　　他們順利地航行，老人把兩手都泡在鹽水裡，想要使頭腦保持清醒。積雲堆得很高，上面還有很多卷雲，老人因此知道微風會吹一整晚。老人每隔一會兒就去看那條魚，確定牠是真的。一個小時過後，就有第一隻鯊魚來攻擊牠。

　　鯊魚的出現並不是偶然。當那片深色的血雲在一哩深的海裡沉澱擴散時，鯊魚就從深海底下冒了出來。牠來得這麼快，不顧一切地劃破藍色的海面，暴露在太陽下。然後牠沉回海裡，開始循著血腥味跟隨小船和魚的航線。

　　有時牠會把血腥味跟丟了，但總是會重新找到，只要嗅到一絲氣味，牠就會執拗地追過去。牠是隻巨大的灰鯖鯊，天生就是海中速度最快的魚類，全身都很優雅，只有下顎除外。

　　牠的背脊和劍魚一樣藍，腹部是銀色的，皮膚光滑細緻。除了大大的下顎之外，牠的體型和劍魚差不多。牠快速游動，下顎目前是緊閉的，就在海面下，高聳的背鰭動也不動的劃過海水。在牠緊閉的雙唇裡面，八排牙齒全部向內傾斜。那些牙齒不像大多數鯊魚一樣呈金字塔狀，而是好像人的手指彎曲如鳥爪的形狀，幾乎和老人的手指一樣長，而且兩邊都像剃刀一樣銳利。這種魚生來就是要吞噬海中所有的魚類，牠們是這麼的敏捷強壯、武器齊全，根本不會碰到敵手。現在牠聞到了更新鮮的氣味，因而加快速度，藍色的背鰭劃開水面。

　　老人看到牠游過來時，就知道那是隻鯊魚，這種傢伙什麼都不怕，想做什麼就會做什麼。他準備好魚叉，繫好繩索，緊盯著鯊魚來到。繩索很短，因為已經割了一段去綁大魚。

　　現在老人的頭腦十分清醒，他意志堅定，但是希望渺茫。好事情都持續不久，他想。在他望著那隻鯊魚逼近時，他又瞥了一眼那條魚。我寧可這是一場夢，他想。我不能阻止牠來攻擊我，但是也許我能給牠點顏色。灰鯖鯊，他想著。你要倒大楣啦。

　　鯊魚迅速地逼近船尾，撲向那條魚時，老人看到牠張開的嘴巴、怪異的眼睛，還有牠咬下靠近尾巴的肉時，牙齒發出的咯嚓聲。鯊魚頭露出水面，牠的背脊也跟著浮現。老人對準鯊魚頭，把魚叉刺進牠兩眼之間與從鼻子伸到背上的線

交叉的地方時，聽見大魚的皮肉撕裂的聲音。牠身上並沒有這些線，只有尖銳的藍色大頭顱和大眼睛，以及會咯嚓咯嚓作響，什麼都吞得進去的下顎。但是那是牠的大腦所在，老人擊中了那裡。他鮮血淋灕的雙手握著一支完好的魚叉，用盡全部的力氣刺進去。他在刺牠的時候並不抱任何希望，只是滿懷著決心和百分之百的敵意。

鯊魚翻了個身，老人看到牠的眼睛已經沒有生氣，但是牠又翻了一次，因而被繩索繞了兩圈。老人知道牠死了，可是鯊魚並不接受這個事實。牠肚皮朝上躺著，尾巴拍擊著水面，下顎咯嚓咯嚓響著，像快艇似的浮游而去，尾巴激出了白色的水花。牠有四分之三的身體浮在水面上，這時繩子繃得很緊，顫動了一下就斷了。老人看著鯊魚在水面上靜躺了一會兒，然後十分緩慢地沉入海中。

「牠咬掉了四十磅的肉。」老人大聲說道。牠也帶走了我的魚叉和全部的繩子，他想。現在我的魚又流血了，一定還會有其他鯊魚過來。

他不忍再去看那條魚，因為牠已經殘缺不全。大魚受到攻擊時，他覺得被攻擊的好像是自己。

可是我殺了攻擊大魚的鯊魚，他心想。牠是我所見過的最大的灰鯖鯊。老天知道，大魚我可看多了。

好事情都持續不久，他想。我現在希望這一切都是夢，我從沒有釣到那條魚，我正單獨一個人躺在鋪著報紙

的床上。

　　「可是人並不是註定要失敗的，」他說，「人可以被毀滅，但不能被打敗。」雖然殺了那條魚我很難過，他想。現在糟糕的時刻來了，卻連支魚叉都沒有。那隻灰鯖鯊很殘酷、很厲害，也很勇猛、很聰明。可是我比牠更聰明。也許沒有，他想。也許我只是武器比牠好。

　　「別再想了，老頭子，」他大聲說，「繼續往這個方向走，等鯊魚來了再看著辦。」

　　可是我一定要想，他想。因為那是我唯一能夠做的。除了想，就是棒球了。不知道了不起的狄馬吉歐喜不喜歡我刺鯊魚頭的手法？那沒什麼大不了的，他想著。誰都做得到。可是，你認不認為我這兩隻手的問題和骨刺一樣，是個很大的障礙？我不知道。我的腳後跟從來沒有出過毛病，除了有一次游泳時踩到刺魟魚，被牠刺了一下，小腿就麻痺了，痛得受不了。

　　「想點愉快的事吧，老頭子，」他說，「現在每過一分鐘你就離家更近。丟掉四十磅肉，船航行起來輕快多了。」

　　他很清楚船航到海潮中會發生什麼事，可是他現在一點辦法也沒有。

　　「有辦法了，」他大聲說，「我可以把刀子綁在槳柄上。」

　　他馬上就去做，把舵夾在腋窩下，用腳踩住帆腳索。

　　「現在，」他說，「我雖然還是個老頭子，但是並不是

沒有武器。」

風變強了，他航行得很順利。老人只看著魚的前半部，恢復了一些希望。

不懷抱希望是很愚蠢的，他想。而且我相信那是種罪過，他心想。問題已經夠多了，還想什麼罪過，何況我對罪過一點都不了解。

我不了解，也不知道是不是要相信罪過。也許殺了那條魚就是罪過，即使我殺牠是為了生存，也為了餵飽許多人。可是這麼說的話，什麼事情都是罪過了。不要去想罪過，現在想這個太遲了，何況有很多人靠這個賺錢，讓他們去想吧。你天生就是要當漁夫，就像魚天生就是要當魚一樣。聖保羅就是個漁夫，了不起的狄馬吉歐的父親也是。

可是老人很喜歡去想那些他遇到過的事情。因為沒有東西可以閱讀，也沒有收音機，他想了很多事情，也繼續思考罪過。你殺那條魚並不只是為了生存，拿牠去換取食物，他想著。你是為了自尊才殺了牠，也因為你是個漁夫。牠活著的時候，你愛牠，牠死了以後你還是愛牠。如果你愛牠，殺牠就不算是罪過。或者是罪加一等？

「你想太多了，老頭子。」他大聲說。

可是那隻灰鯖鯊你就殺得很高興，他想。他和你一樣，靠著捕捉活魚過日子。牠不吃腐肉，也不會像一些鯊魚一樣有貪婪的食慾。牠既美麗又高貴，什麼都不怕。

「我殺牠是為了自衛，」老人大聲說。「而且殺得很

漂亮。」

何況，他想，所有東西都是以某種方式去殺自己以外的東西。捕魚養活了我，同樣也快把我害死了。那孩子使我活下去。我還是不要太過於欺騙自己。

他靠在船邊，從大魚被鯊魚咬破的地方扯下一片肉，放進嘴裡咀嚼，嚐嚐牠的肉質和鮮味。肉質緊緻多汁，就像其他的肉，但不是紅色的。肉裡面沒有筋，他知道可以在市場上賣到最高的價錢。但是沒有辦法使血腥味不在海裡散發，老人知道最糟糕的狀況就要發生了。

風穩定地吹著，風向已經稍微偏往東北，老人知道這表示風不會平息。老人遙望前方，看不見任何帆影、船體，或汽船冒出來的煙。只有飛魚在船頭分往兩旁跳躍，以及一叢叢的黃色馬尾藻。他連一隻鳥都沒有看到。

船行駛了兩個小時，老人在這段時間都在船尾歇息，有時候撕一點馬林魚肉來嚼，努力休息，增強體力。這時他看到了兩隻鯊魚中首先露出水面的一隻。

「啊呀！」他大叫。這兩個字是沒辦法說明的，也許那只是一個人感覺到兩手被釘子釘在木頭上時，不由自主發出來的聲音。

「加拉諾鯊！」他用西班牙語大叫。他看到第一片鰭後面跟著第二片鰭，從三角形的褐色鰭和搖擺的尾巴認出牠們是有鏟形鼻子的雙髻鯊。牠們聞到了血腥味非常興奮，因為餓昏了頭，一下子把氣味跟丟了，一下子又興高采烈地找到

氣味。牠們正在不斷地逼近。

　　老人把帆腳索綁緊，再固定舵柄，拿起綁著刀子的槳柄。他盡可能輕輕地舉槳，因為他的手痛得不聽使喚。他輕輕伸展手掌，然後又握緊，以使雙手放鬆。此時他用力握住槳柄，忍受疼痛，絕不退縮。他望著鯊魚過來，看到牠們寬大扁平、像鏟尖的頭顱，以及末端泛白的寬闊胸鰭。牠們是令人憎厭的鯊魚，身上有惡臭，也是吃腐肉的殺手，餓的時候連槳或舵都咬。就是這種鯊魚會在烏龜浮到水面睡覺時咬掉牠們的腳和鰭肢，而且會在很餓時攻擊游泳的人，即使那個人沒有魚的血腥味或黏液也是一樣。

　　「啊呀，」老人說，「加拉諾鯊。來吧，加拉諾鯊。」

　　牠們來了，但是來的方式不像之前那隻灰鯖鯊。有一隻轉了個圈，在船底下消失。牠拉扯大魚時，老人感覺得到船在晃動。另一隻用牠細長的黃眼睛瞪著老人，然後迅速游過來，張開半圓形的下顎，撲向大魚之前被咬過的地方。牠褐色的頭頂和背脊上的線很清楚，那是腦部與脊髓交會的地方。老人把綁著刀子的槳刺進那個交會點，然後抽回來再刺進牠貓一般的黃眼睛。鯊魚放開大魚，沉入海裡，臨死時還把咬下的肉吞進肚裡。

　　另一隻鯊魚還在船底下蹂躪那條魚，因此小船仍在搖晃。老人放開帆腳索，好讓船打橫，露出底下的鯊魚。他一看到鯊魚，就靠到船邊，朝牠刺去。他只擊中鯊魚的肉，而鯊魚皮很厚，要刺進去很困難。這一用力不僅震痛了手，連

　肩膀也很痛。但是鯊魚很快又把頭露出來，就在牠的鼻子浮出水面要去進攻大魚時，老人又直接刺向他平坦的頭頂中央。老人抽出刀子，又在同樣的位置刺了一刀。牠依舊緊鎖著上下顎，咬著大魚不放，老人一刀戳進牠的左眼。鯊魚仍然不肯鬆口。

　「還不夠？」老人說，把刀子刺進脊椎骨和腦部之間。這次很容易，他感覺到軟骨斷裂。老人把槳倒過來，用刀刃去掰開鯊魚的下顎。他扭轉刀刃，終於使鯊魚鬆口時，他說：「滾開，加拉諾鯊。沉到一哩深的地方見你的朋友去，或者牠是你媽媽。」

　老人擦擦刀刃，把槳放下來。接著他拾起帆腳索，風漲

滿了帆，讓小船朝正確的航道駛去。

「有四分之一被牠們糟蹋掉了，而且是最好的肉，」他大聲說，「真希望這是一場夢，希望我沒有釣到牠。魚啊，我很抱歉，這一切都錯了。」他沉默下來，已經不忍去看那條魚了。魚的血液已經沖刷乾淨，他看到牠和鏡子背面一樣的銀色，條紋依然清晰。

「魚啊，我不應該出海這麼遠，」他說，「對你，對我都沒有意義。魚啊，我很抱歉。」

現在他在心裡對自己說。看看綁刀子的繩子是不是要斷了。還有叫你的手準備好，因為還有更多鯊魚要來。

「希望我有塊石頭可以磨刀，」老人檢查綁在槳柄上的繩子後說，「我應該帶一塊石頭來。」很多東西你都應該帶來，他想著。可是你偏偏沒有帶來，老頭子。現在可不是去想缺少什麼東西的時候。你倒是應該想想怎麼利用現有的東西。

「你給我出了很多好主意，」他大聲說，「可是我聽膩了。」

他把舵柄夾在腋下，在小船繼續往前行時，把雙手都浸在水裡。

「天知道後面那隻鯊魚幹掉了多少肉，」他說，「不過船現在輕多了。」他不忍去想像被鯊魚撕爛的魚肚子。他知道每次鯊魚猛烈晃動時，就有一塊肉被撕開。這條魚為所有

鯊魚開了一條路徑，好像海上寬廣的高速公路。

　　這條魚可以讓一個人足足吃一個冬天，他想。別想那個了，好好休息，把你的手調養好，才能去保護剩下來的部分。和海裡散佈的氣味相比，我手上的血腥味根本不算什麼。何況我的手沒有流很多血，傷口不成問題，流血卻可以讓左手不抽筋。

　　現在我要想什麼呢？他想。沒什麼可想的。我什麼都不要去想，等著下一批鯊魚來就好了。希望這一切真的是夢，他想。可是誰知道呢，也許事情會轉好。

　　接著來了一隻落單的雙髻鯊，游過來的模樣就像隻衝向食槽的豬。當然豬的嘴巴沒有牠那麼大，大得連人的頭都進得去。老人先讓牠去咬大魚，然後舉起槳上的刀子，往牠的腦門刺去。可是鯊魚翻滾時猛然後退，刀刃頓時斷裂。

　　老人在掌舵的地方坐定。他甚至不去看那隻大鯊魚逐漸沉進水中，牠起先展現出實際的身長，然後越變越小，最後變成一丁點。這原本都能讓老人看得入迷，可是這回他連看都不想看。

　　「我現在還有魚鉤，」他說，「可是魚鉤沒什麼用處。我有兩把槳、舵柄和短棍。」

　　牠們可把我打敗了，他想。我太老了，沒辦法用棍子把鯊魚打死。可是我要試試看，只要我有槳和短棍、舵柄。

　　他再次把手泡在水中。已經快接近黃昏，眼前除了海和天之外，什麼也看不見。空中的風比之前更大了，他希望很

The Old Man and the Sea

快就會看到陸地。

「你累了，老頭子，」他說，「你的內心累壞了。」

即將日落時，鯊魚再度前來攻擊。

老人看到褐色的鰭順著大魚在水中產生的寬廣路徑來到。牠們並不在血腥味中探索，而是並肩而行，一路奔向小船。

他把舵固定好，繫牢帆腳索，手探到船尾底下拿木棍。那是從一把斷槳上鋸下來的柄，大約有兩呎半長。因為有個把手，只能用一隻手去抓。他用右手緊緊握住，一邊繃緊他的手，一邊盯著鯊魚游過來。這兩隻都是加拉諾鯊。

我必須讓第一隻先咬一口，再往牠的鼻頭或頭頂敲下去，他想。

兩隻鯊魚一起逼近，他看到較接近他的那一隻嘴巴大張，一頭埋進大魚的銀色腹側裡。他高舉木棍，重重地打在鯊魚寬闊的頭頂上。木棍落下來時，他感覺到結實的彈力，但同時也感覺到骨頭的堅硬。在鯊魚從大魚身上滑落時，他再次用力擊打牠的鼻頭。

另一隻鯊魚一直忽隱忽現，現在又張著大嘴過來了。牠衝向大魚，闔起下顎時，老人看見一塊塊白色的魚肉從牠的嘴漏出來。他用力朝牠打去，卻只打中牠的頭，鯊魚看著他，仍然把咬在嘴裡的肉撕下來。牠游開去把肉嚥下時，老人再次用木棍敲擊牠，卻只感覺到厚實的彈力。

「來吧，加拉諾鯊，」老人說，「再來。」

鯊魚衝了過來，老人在牠閉起下顎時打他。他盡可能把木棍舉高，再狠狠敲下去。這回他感覺擊中了牠後腦的骨頭。他又往同樣的位置敲了一次，鯊魚有氣無力地撕下一塊肉，從大魚身上滑落。

老人注意盯著牠，看牠會不會再回來，可是兩隻鯊魚都沒有出現。然後他看到有一隻在水面上兜圈子，而另外一隻連鰭都沒有看見。

我不指望能殺死牠們，他想。我年輕時是有這個能耐，不過我已經使牠們受了重傷，那兩隻都不會覺得好過。如果我可以用兩手握住棍子，一定可以打死第一隻。即使是現在也行，他想。

他不想去看那條魚，他知道魚身已經毀掉一半了。在他和鯊魚搏鬥時，太陽已經落下去了。

「天很快就要黑了，」他說，「我就會看到哈瓦那的亮光。如果我太偏向東方，也會看到某個沙灘的燈火。」

現在不會離岸邊太遠了，他想。希望沒有人太擔心。當然，只有那個孩子會擔心。可是他一定對我有信心。許多年紀較大的漁夫會擔心，其他許多人也會。我住的村子很不錯。

他不能再跟牠說話了，因為魚損毀得很厲害。他忽然想起一件事。

「半條魚啊，」他說，「你原本是條全魚。很抱歉我出

海太遠,把我們倆都毀了。可是我們殺了很多隻鯊魚,就你和我,還傷了許多隻。老魚,你殺死過多少隻呢?你頭上那根長矛可不是白長的。」

他喜歡去想那條魚。如果牠可以自由游動,不曉得會怎麼對付鯊魚。我應該把牠的長喙砍下來,用它去和鯊魚對抗。可是船上沒有斧頭,也沒有刀子。

但如果有工具,我可以把它綁在槳柄上,那會是多麼美麗的武器啊。那樣子我們就能一起和牠們作戰。如果牠們晚上又來了,你會怎麼辦?你能怎麼辦?

「和牠們鬥,」他說,「我會和牠們鬥到死掉為止。」

可是,現在四周都黑了,沒有亮光,也沒有燈火,只有風和穩定前行的船,老人覺得他可能已經死了。他雙手交握,摸摸掌心。手還沒有死,他只需藉著手掌的開合,就能感覺到生命的苦痛。他把背靠在船頭上,知道自己還沒死,肩膀告訴他了。

我答應要在釣到魚時唸祈禱文,他想起來,可是我現在太累了,沒辦法唸。我最好把布袋拿出來披在肩上。

他躺在船尾,掌著舵,等待天空出現亮光。我還有半條魚,他想。也許我有帶回半條魚的運氣。我總該有點運氣。不,他說。你出海那麼遠,已經把你的好運氣搞砸了。

「別傻了,」他大聲說,「保持清醒,掌好舵。也許你還有很多好運氣。」

「如果有什麼地方在賣好運氣,我還真想買一些。」

他說。

　　我要用什麼來買呢？他問自己。我能用失去的魚叉、斷裂的刀子和兩隻受了傷的手去買嗎？

　　「也許可以，」他說，「你曾經用出海八十四天來買，他們也幾乎賣給你了。」

　　我不應該再胡思亂想了，他想。運氣出現的形式有很多種，誰認得出她呢？不管是什麼形式，我都願意買一些，而且不討價還價。希望我能看到城市的亮光，他心想。我的願望太多了，可是那是我現在最希望的。老人盡量使自己在掌舵時舒服些。他從身體上的疼痛知道，自己還沒有死。

　　大概在晚上十點時，老人看到了城市的燈火反射的亮光。起初只是隱約可見，好像月亮升上天空之前的微光，後來隔著越來越強的風產生的洶湧海域，變得清楚可見了。他駛入了這反光的圈子，心想他很快就要駛到墨西哥灣流的邊緣了。

　　總算結束了，他想。鯊魚可能還會再來攻擊我。可是人在黑暗中，又沒有武器，我能怎麼辦呢？

　　現在他渾身僵硬痠痛，隨著夜裡的寒氣，傷口和身上所有勞累過度的部位都在發痛。希望我不必再拚命了，他想。我真的非常希望不必再拚命了。

　　但是，到了午夜他又得拚命了，而這一次他知道，再怎麼拚命都沒用了。牠們成群結隊而來，他只看得到牠們的鰭在水中畫出的線條，還有身體在撲向大魚時的粼光。

老人用木棍打牠們的頭，聽到牠們在船底下搶食時下顎的咯嚓聲和小船搖晃的聲音。他不顧一切地朝任何聽得見或感覺得到的地方打去，接著他感覺到有什麼攫住了棍子，棍子就不見了。

他把舵從舵樁上扯下來，用雙手握住，一次又一次地往下劈敲擊打。但是鯊魚群已經竄到船頭，一條接一條，或是成群湧來，撕去一片片的肉塊，那些肉塊在牠們轉個身要再撲過來時在水裡閃爍。

最後，有一隻鯊魚直撲魚頭，他知道一切都完了。他用舵往鯊魚的頭上劈下去，牠的顎正卡在大魚那又重又硬，實在咬不下的頭上。他一次又一次的劈打，聽見舵柄斷裂的聲音，接著就用殘餘的木棒朝鯊魚身上戳下去。他感覺到舵柄戳進去了，也知道木棒的裂口很尖銳，因此又往裡頭刺。鯊魚鬆開了嘴，翻滾而去。那是整群中的最後一隻。這裡已經沒有東西給牠們吃了。

老人幾乎喘不過氣來，他覺得口中有種奇怪的味道，帶點銅味，而且甜甜的。這令他擔心了一下子。但是那味道並不太重。

他在海裡吐了一口唾沫，然後說：「吃吧，加拉諾鯊，去做個殺人的夢吧！」

他知道他終於被打敗了，沒法補救了。他回到船尾，發現斷裂的舵柄還插得進舵孔，足以讓他掌控方向。他把布袋圍在肩膀上，將小船開上航道。他現在航行得很輕鬆，什麼

老人與海

都不想，也沒有任何一種情緒。他什麼都不在乎了，只是盡可能妥善地操縱小船，把船開回家鄉的港灣。在深夜，鯊魚多次攻擊骨骸，就像有人會去撿拾桌上的麵包屑一樣。老人一點都不理會牠們，對任何事情都漠不關心，除了掌舵之外。他只注意到沒有船邊沉重的負荷之後，船走起來是多麼的輕快順利。

她真是條好船，他想。她很結實，沒有任何損傷，除了舵柄以外，而那要更換很容易。

他感覺到已經航進灣流，也可以看到沿岸海灘聚落的燈光。他曉得自己所在的位置，要回家不成問題了。

不管怎樣，風是我們的朋友，他想。他又補充說，有時候是。而大海裡面有我們的朋友和敵人。床呢，他想。床是我的朋友。就是床，他想著，床是個了不得的東西。被打敗很輕鬆，他想。我從來不知道是這麼的輕鬆。是什麼把你打敗了呢，他想。

「什麼都不是，」他大聲說，「只是我出海太遠了。」

他航進那個小港口時，露天酒吧的燈光已經熄滅，他知道所有人都上床睡覺了。風慢慢刮起，現在已經相當強了。然而，港口很安靜。他划進岩石下面的一小片沙灘。沒有人幫他的忙，他只好自己把船盡量往上划。然後他跨出來，把船繫在岩石上。

他卸下桅桿，把帆捲起來綑好，扛在肩上，開始往上爬。直到這時候，他才知道自己有多麼疲倦。他停了一會

兒，回過頭，在街燈的反射下，碩大的魚尾在船尾的後面直直翹起。他看見背脊骨光禿禿的白色線條，還有帶著尖喙的漆黑頭顱。除了骨架，什麼都沒有。

他又開始爬，爬到頂上時滑倒了。他把桅杆橫在肩上，在地上躺了一會兒。他努力想要站起來，可是實在太困難了，只好坐在那裡，扛著桅杆，望著馬路。一隻貓在遠處經過，忙著去辦自己的事。老人一直盯著牠，然後就只是望著馬路。

最後他把桅杆放下，站了起來，再拎起桅杆，把它扛在肩上，開始上路。在抵達小屋之前，他總共坐下來休息了五次。

進了屋子，他把桅杆靠在牆邊。在黑暗中，他摸到一瓶水，喝了一口，然後在床上躺下來，拉起毯子蓋在肩膀、背部和腳上，臉朝下挨著報紙，雙臂直伸，掌心朝上，就這樣睡著了。

早晨，男孩在門口往屋內張望時，老人還在熟睡。風刮得很大，停泊的小船不能出海，所以男孩起得比較晚，然後就像每天早晨一樣，來到老人的小屋。他看著老人呼吸，注意到老人的雙手，就開始哭了。他安靜地走出去，想帶點咖啡來，一路上哭個不停。

許多漁夫圍著小船，觀看著綁在船邊的東西，其中一個人還捲著褲管站在水裡，用釣索在量那死魚的殘骸。

男孩並沒有走下去。他之前就下去過了，有個漁夫在幫

他看管那艘船。

「他怎麼樣？」一名漁夫大叫。

「在睡覺，」男孩喊道。他不介意他們看到他在哭。「大家都不要去吵他。」

「牠從鼻子到尾巴足足有十八呎長！」測量的漁夫喊道。

「我相信。」男孩說。

他跑到露天酒吧，要了一罐咖啡。

「要熱的，多放些牛奶和糖。」

「還要不要別的？」

「不了，等一下再看看他吃得下什麼。」

The Old Man and the Sea

　「那條魚真是不得了，」老闆說，「從來沒有見過那麼大的魚。你昨天捕到的那兩隻也不賴。」

　「我的魚，見鬼去。」男孩一說，又開始哭了。

　「你要不要喝點什麼？」老闆問。

　「不要，」男孩說，「跟他們說，不要去打擾桑地亞哥。我要回去了。」

　「代我向他表達遺憾。」

　「謝謝。」男孩說。

　男孩帶著一罐熱咖啡來到老人的小屋，坐在旁邊等他醒來。老人有一度好像要醒過來了，卻又沉沉睡去。男孩只好走到對街去借木柴來熱咖啡。

　老人終於醒了。

　「別坐起來，」男孩說，「喝下這個。」他在杯子裡倒了些咖啡。

　老人接過杯子，喝下咖啡。

　「牠們把我打敗了，馬諾林，」他說，「牠們確實把我打敗了！」

　「牠沒有把你打敗，那條魚沒有。」

　「對，沒錯。是後來才打敗的。」

　「佩德利克在照顧那艘船和船具。你要怎麼處置那個魚頭？」

　「叫佩德利克把它剁下來，用來做捕魚的陷阱好了。」

　「那根長嘴呢？」

「你要的話就給你。」

「我要，」男孩說。「現在我們要為別的事情計畫一下。」

「他們尋找過我嗎？」

「當然，海岸警備隊和飛機都出動了。」

「海洋太大，船又太小，很難看到。」老人說。他注意到，有講話的對象是多麼愉快的事，比自言自語或對大海說話好多了。「我很想你，」他說，「你捕到什麼了？」

「第一天一條，第二天一條，第三天兩條。」

「太好了。」

「我們現在又可以一起捕魚了。」

「不行，我的運氣不好。我的運氣好不起來了。」

「去他的運氣，」男孩說，「我會給你帶來好運。」

「你的家人會怎麼說？」

「我才不管呢。我昨天捕到兩條了。我們現在要一起捕魚，因為我還有很多東西要學。」

「我們得弄一根長矛，上船一定要帶著。你可以從舊的福特汽車找個彈簧做矛頭。我們可以拿到瓜納巴科亞的工廠磨一磨。一定要很利，但是不能用火燒，免得容易斷裂。我的刀子斷了。」

「我會幫你找一把刀，再把彈簧磨一磨。這種大風要刮幾天呢？」

「可能要三天，也可能更久。」

「我會把所有東西都準備好，」男孩說，「你倒是要把

手治好，老伯。」

「我知道怎麼治療手。昨晚我吐了一些怪東西，覺得胸口好像有什麼東西破掉了。」

「那也要治好，」男孩說，「躺下來，老伯，我去拿你那件乾淨的襯衫，再拿一些吃的來。」

「順便帶幾張我不在這幾天的報紙。」老人說。

「你一定要快點好起來，我有很多東西要學，你全部都要教給我。你吃了多少苦啊？」

「很多。」老人說。

「我去幫你帶吃的和報紙，」男孩說，「好好休息，老伯，我會去藥房弄點東西給你抹在手上。」

「別忘了告訴佩德利可，魚頭要給他。」

「我不會忘記。」

男孩出了門，沿著碎珊瑚礁舖的馬路走下去時，再度哭了起來。

那天下午，露天酒吧來了許多觀光客。一個女人從空啤酒罐和死梭魚之間看到一根又大又長的白色背脊骨，後端還連著巨大的魚尾，隨著浪潮晃來晃去。港口外面，東風強勁地吹刮，使海面湧起波濤。

「那是什麼？」她問一個侍者，指著那條長長的背脊骨，那現在只是個垃圾，等著潮水把它帶走。

「提布隆，」侍者接著改以不準確的英語說，「鯊魚，」想要描述事情的經過。

「我不知道鯊魚尾巴的形狀那麼美麗、精巧。」

「我也不知道。」她的男伴說。

在道路另一頭的小屋裡，老人又沉沉睡去。他的臉依然朝下，男孩就在旁邊望著他。老人夢見了獅子。

The Old Man and the Sea

老人與海

He was an old man who fished alone in a skiff in the Gulf Stream and he had gone eighty-four days now without taking a fish. In the first forty days a boy had been with him. But after forty days without a fish the boy's parents had told him that the old man was now definitely and finally salao, which is the worst form of unlucky, and the boy had gone at their orders in another boat which caught three good fish the first week. It made the boy sad to see the old man come in each day with his skiff empty and he always went down to help him carry either the coiled lines or the gaff and harpoon and the sail that was furled around the mast. The sail was patched with flour sacks and, furled, it looked like the flag of permanent defeat.

The old man was thin and gaunt with deep wrinkles in the back of his neck. The brown blotches of the benevolent skin cancer the sun brings from its reflection on the tropic sea were on his cheeks. The blotches ran well down the sides of his face and his hands had the deep-creased scars from handling heavy fish on the cords. But none of these scars were fresh. They were as old as erosions in a fishless desert.

Everything about him was old except his eyes and they were the same color as the sea and were cheerful and undefeated.

"Santiago," the boy said to him as they climbed the bank from where the skiff was hauled up. "I could go with you again. We've made some money."

The old man had taught the boy to fish and the boy loved him.

"No," the old man said. "You're with a lucky boat. Stay with them."

"But remember how you went eighty-seven days without fish and then we caught big ones every day for three weeks."

"I remember," the old man said. "I know you did not leave me because you doubted."

"It was papa made me leave. I am a boy and I must obey him."

"I know," the old man said. "It is quite normal."

"He hasn't much faith."

"No," the old man said. "But we have. Haven't we?"

"Yes," the boy said. "Can I offer you a beer on the Terrace and then we'll take the stuff home."

"Why not?" the old man said. "Between fishermen."

They sat on the Terrace and many of the fishermen made fun of the old man and he was not angry. Others, of the older fishermen, looked at him and were sad. But they did not show it and they spoke politely about the current and the depths they had drifted their lines at and the steady good weather and of what they had seen. The successful fishermen of that day were already in and had butchered their marlin out and carried them laid full length across two planks, with two men staggering at the end of each plank, to the fish house where they waited for the ice truck to carry them to the

market in Havana. Those who had caught sharks had taken them to the shark factory on the other side of the cove where they were hoisted on a block and tackle, their livers removed, their fins cut off and their hides skinned out and their flesh cut into strips for salting.

When the wind was in the east a smell came across the harbour from the shark factory; but today there was only the faint edge of the odour because the wind had backed into the north and then dropped off and it was pleasant and sunny on the Terrace.

"Santiago," the boy said.

"Yes," the old man said. He was holding his glass and thinking of many years ago.

"Can I go out to get sardines for you for tomorrow?"

"No. Go and play baseball. I can still row and Rogelio will throw the net."

"I would like to go. If I cannot fish with you, I would like to serve in some way."

"You bought me a beer," the old man said. "You are already a man."

"How old was I when you first took me in a boat?"

"Five and you nearly were killed when I brought the fish in too green and he nearly tore the boat to pieces. Can you remember?"

"I can remember the tail slapping and banging and the thwart breaking and the noise of the clubbing. I can remember you throwing me into the bow where the wet coiled lines were and feeling the whole boat shiver and the noise of you clubbing him like chopping a tree down and the sweet blood smell all over me."

"Can you really remember that or did I just tell it to you?"

"I remember everything from when we first went together."

The old man looked at him with his sun-burned, confident loving eyes.

"If you were my boy I'd take you out and gamble," he said. "But you are your father's and your mother's and you are in a lucky boat."

"May I get the sardines? I know where I can get four baits too."

"I have mine left from today. I put them in salt in the box."

"Let me get four fresh ones."

"One," the old man said. His hope and his confidence had never gone. But now they were freshening as when the breeze rises.

"Two," the boy said.

"Two," the old man agreed. "You didn't steal them?"

"I would," the boy said. "But I bought these."

"Thank you," the old man said. He was too simple to wonder when he had attained humility. But he knew he had attained it and he knew it was not disgraceful and it carried no loss of true pride.

"Tomorrow is going to be a good day with this current," he said.

"Where are you going?" the boy asked.

"Far out to come in when the wind shifts. I want to be out before it is light."

"I'll try to get him to work far out," the boy said. "Then if you hook something truly big we can come to your aid."

"He does not like to work too far out."

"No," the boy said. "But I will see something that he cannot see such as a bird working and get him to come out after dolphin."

"Are his eyes that bad?"

"He is almost blind."

"It is strange," the old man said. "He never went turtle-ing. That is what kills the eyes."

"But you went turtle-ing for years off the Mosquito Coast and your eyes are good."

"I am a strange old man."

"But are you strong enough now for a truly big fish?"

"I think so. And there are many tricks."

"Let us take the stuff home," the boy said. "So I can get the cast net and go after the sardines."

They picked up the gear from the boat. The old man carried the mast on his shoulder and the boy carried the wooden box with the coiled, hard-braided brown lines, the gaff and the harpoon with its shaft. The box with the baits was under the stern of the skiff along with the club that was used to subdue the big fish when they were brought alongside. No one would steal from the old man but it was better to take the sail and the heavy lines home as the dew was bad for them and, though he was quite sure no local people would steal from him, the old man thought that a gaff and a harpoon were needless temptations to leave in a boat.

They walked up the road together to the old man's shack

and went in through its open door. The old man leaned the mast with its wrapped sail against the wall and the boy put the box and the other gear beside it. The mast was nearly as long as the one room of the shack. The shack was made of the tough bud-shields of the royal palm which are called guano and in it there was a bed, a table, one chair, and a place on the dirt floor to cook with charcoal. On the brown walls of the flattened, overlapping leaves of the sturdy fibered guano there was a picture in color of the Sacred Heart of Jesus and another of the Virgin of Cobre. These were relics of his wife. Once there had been a tinted photograph of his wife on the wall but he had taken it down because it made him too lonely to see it and it was on the shelf in the corner under his clean shirt.

"What do you have to eat?" the boy asked.

"A pot of yellow rice with fish. Do you want some?"

"No. I will eat at home. Do you want me to make the fire?"

"No. I will make it later on. Or I may eat the rice cold."

"May I take the cast net?"

"Of course."

There was no cast net and the boy remembered when they had sold it. But they went through this fiction every day. There was no pot of yellow rice and fish and the boy knew this too.

"Eighty-five is a lucky number," the old man said. "How

would you like to see me bring one in that dressed out over a thousand pounds?"

"I'll get the cast net and go for sardines. Will you sit in the sun in the doorway?"

"Yes. I have yesterday's paper and I will read the baseball."

The boy did not know whether yesterday's paper was a fiction too. But the old man brought it out from under the bed.

"Perico gave it to me at the bodega," he explained.

"I'll be back when I have the sardines. I'll keep yours and mine together on ice and we can share them in the morning. When I come back you can tell me about the baseball."

"The Yankees cannot lose."

"But I fear the Indians of Cleveland."

"Have faith in the Yankees my son. Think of the great DiMaggio."

"I fear both the Tigers of Detroit and the Indians of Cleveland."

"Be careful or you will fear even the Reds of Cincinnati and the White Sox of Chicago."

"You study it and tell me when I come back."

"Do you think we should buy a terminal of the lottery with an eighty-five? Tomorrow is the eighty-fifth day."

"We can do that," the boy said. "But what about the eighty-seven of your great record?"

"It could not happen twice. Do you think you can find an eighty-five?"

"I can order one."

"One sheet. That's two dollars and a half. Who can we borrow that from?"

"That's easy. I can always borrow two dollars and a half."

"I think perhaps I can too. But I try not to borrow. First you borrow. Then you beg."

"Keep warm old man," the boy said. "Remember we are in September."

"The month when the great fish come," the old man said. "Anyone can be a fisherman in May."

"I go now for the sardines," the boy said.

When the boy came back the old man was asleep in the chair and the sun was down. The boy took the old army blanket off the bed and spread it over the back of the chair and over the old man's shoulders. They were strange shoulders, still powerful although very old, and the neck was still strong too and the creases did not show so much when the old man was asleep and his head fallen forward. His shirt had been patched so many times that it was like the sail and the patches were faded to many different shades by the sun. The old man's head was very old though and with his eyes closed there was no life in his face. The newspaper lay across his knees and the weight of his arm held it there in the evening breeze. He was barefooted.

The boy left him there and when he came back the old man was still asleep.

"Wake up old man," the boy said and put his hand on one of the old man's knees.

The old man opened his eyes and for a moment he was coming back from a long way away. Then he smiled.

"What have you got?" he asked.

"Supper," said the boy. "We're going to have supper."

"I'm not very hungry."

"Come on and eat. You can't fish and not eat."

"I have," the old man said getting up and taking the newspaper and folding it. Then he started to fold the blanket.

"Keep the blanket around you," the boy said. "You'll not fish without eating while I'm alive."

"Then live a long time and take care of yourself," the old man said. "What are we eating?"

"Black beans and rice, fried bananas, and some stew."

The boy had brought them in a two-decker metal container from the Terrace. The two sets of knives and forks and spoons were in his pocket with a paper napkin wrapped around each set.

"Who gave this to you?"

"Martin. The owner."

"I must thank him."

"I thanked him already," the boy said. "You don't need to thank him."

"I'll give him the belly meat of a big fish," the old man said. "Has he done this for us more than once?"

"I think so."

"I must give him something more than the belly meat then. He is very thoughtful for us."

"He sent two beers."

"I like the beer in cans best."

"I know. But this is in bottles, Hatuey beer, and I take back the bottles."

"That's very kind of you," the old man said. "Should we eat?"

"I've been asking you to," the boy told him gently. "I have not wished to open the container until you were ready."

"I'm ready now," the old man said. "I only needed time to wash."

Where did you wash? the boy thought. The village water supply was two streets down the road. I must have water here for him, the boy thought, and soap and a good towel. Why am I so thoughtless? I must get him another shirt and a jacket for the winter and some sort of shoes and another blanket.

"Your stew is excellent," the old man said.

"Tell me about the baseball," the boy asked him.

"In the American League it is the Yankees as I said," the old man said happily.

"They lost today," the boy told him.

"That means nothing. The great DiMaggio is himself again."

"They have other men on the team."

"Naturally. But he makes the difference. In the other league, between Brooklyn and Philadelphia I must take Brooklyn. But then I think of Dick Sisler and those great drives in the old park."

"There was nothing ever like them. He hits the longest ball I have ever seen."

"Do you remember when he used to come to the Terrace? I wanted to take him fishing but I was too timid to ask him. Then I asked you to ask him and you were too timid."

"I know. It was a great mistake. He might have gone with us. Then we would have that for all of our lives."

"I would like to take the great DiMaggio fishing," the old man said. "They say his father was a fisherman. Maybe he was as poor as we are and would understand."

"The great Sisler's father was never poor and he, the father, was playing in the big leagues when he was my age."

"When I was your age I was before the mast on a square rigged ship that ran to Africa and I have seen lions on the beaches in the evening."

"I know. You told me."

"Should we talk about Africa or about baseball?"

"Baseball I think," the boy said. "Tell me about the great John J. McGraw." He said Jota for J.

"He used to come to the Terrace sometimes too in the

older days. But he was rough and harsh-spoken and difficult when he was drinking. His mind was on horses as well as baseball. At least he carried lists of horses at all times in his pocket and frequently spoke the names of horses on the telephone."

"He was a great manager," the boy said. "My father thinks he was the greatest."

"Because he came here the most times," the old man said. "If Durocher had continued to come here each year your father would think him the greatest manager."

"Who is the greatest manager, really, Luque or Mike Gonzalez?"

"I think they are equal."

"And the best fisherman is you."

"No. I know others better."

"Qué va," the boy said. "There are many good fishermen and some great ones. But there is only you."

"Thank you. You make me happy. I hope no fish will come along so great that he will prove us wrong."

"There is no such fish if you are still strong as you say."

"I may not be as strong as I think," the old man said. "But I know many tricks and I have resolution."

"You ought to go to bed now so that you will be fresh in the morning. I will take the things back to the Terrace."

"Good night then. I will wake you in the morning."

"You're my alarm clock," the boy said.

"Age is my alarm clock," the old man said. "Why do old men wake so early? Is it to have one longer day?"

"I don't know," the boy said. "All I know is that young boys sleep late and hard."

"I can remember it," the old man said. "I'll waken you in time."

"I do not like for him to waken me. It is as though I were inferior."

"I know."

"Sleep well, old man."

The boy went out. They had eaten with no light on the table and the old man took off his trousers and went to bed in the dark. He rolled his trousers up to make a pillow, putting the newspaper inside them. He rolled himself in the blanket and slept on the other old newspapers that covered the springs of the bed.

He was asleep in a short time and he dreamed of Africa when he was a boy and the long golden beaches and the white beaches, so white they hurt your eyes, and the high capes and the great brown mountains. He lived along that coast now every night and in his dreams he heard the surf roar and saw the native boats come riding through it. He smelled the tar and oakum of the deck as he slept and he smelled the smell of Africa that the land breeze brought at morning.

Usually when he smelled the land breeze he woke up and dressed to go and wake the boy. But tonight the smell of the

land breeze came very early and he knew it was too early in his dream and went on dreaming to see the white peaks of the Islands rising from the sea and then he dreamed of the different harbours and roadsteads of the Canary Islands.

He no longer dreamed of storms, nor of women, nor of great occurrences, nor of great fish, nor fights, nor contests of strength, nor of his wife. He only dreamed of places now and of the lions on the beach. They played like young cats in the dusk and he loved them as he loved the boy. He never dreamed about the boy. He simply woke, looked out the open door at the moon and unrolled his trousers and put them on. He urinated outside the shack and then went up the road to wake the boy. He was shivering with the morning cold. But he knew he would shiver himself warm and that soon he would be rowing.

The door of the house where the boy lived was unlocked and he opened it and walked in quietly with his bare feet. The boy was asleep on a cot in the first room and the old man could see him clearly with the light that came in from the dying moon. He took hold of one foot gently and held it until the boy woke and turned and looked at him. The old man nodded and the boy took his trousers from the chair by the bed and, sitting on the bed, pulled them on.

The old man went out the door and the boy came after him. He was sleepy and the old man put his arm across his shoulders and said, "I am sorry."

"Qué va," the boy said. "It is what a man must do."

They walked down the road to the old man's shack and all along the road, in the dark, barefoot men were moving, carrying the masts of their boats.

When they reached the old man's shack the boy took the rolls of line in the basket and the harpoon and gaff and the old man carried the mast with the furled sail on his shoulder.

"Do you want coffee?" the boy asked.

"We'll put the gear in the boat and then get some."

They had coffee from condensed milk cans at an early morning place that served fishermen.

"How did you sleep old man?" the boy asked. He was waking up now although it was still hard for him to leave his sleep.

"Very well, Manolin," the old man said. "I feel confident today."

"So do I," the boy said. "Now I must get your sardines and mine and your fresh baits. He brings our gear himself. He never wants anyone to carry anything."

"We're different," the old man said. "I let you carry things when you were five years old."

"I know it," the boy said. "I'll be right back. Have another coffee. We have credit here."

He walked off, bare-footed on the coral rocks, to the ice house where the baits were stored.

The old man drank his coffee slowly. It was all he would

have all day and he knew that he should take it. For a long time now eating had bored him and he never carried a lunch. He had a bottle of water in the bow of the skiff and that was all he needed for the day.

The boy was back now with the sardines and the two baits wrapped in a newspaper and they went down the trail to the skiff, feeling the pebbled sand under their feet, and lifted the skiff and slid her into the water.

"Good luck old man."

"Good luck," the old man said. He fitted the rope lashings of the oars onto the thole pins and, leaning forward against the thrust of the blades in the water, he began to row out of the harbour in the dark. There were other boats from the other beaches going out to sea and the old man heard the dip and push of their oars even though he could not see them now the moon was below the hills.

Sometimes someone would speak in a boat. But most of the boats were silent except for the dip of the oars. They spread apart after they were out of the mouth of the harbour and each one headed for the part of the ocean where he hoped to find fish. The old man knew he was going far out and he left the smell of the land behind and rowed out into the clean early morning smell of the ocean. He saw the phosphorescence of the Gulf weed in the water as he rowed over the part of the ocean that the fishermen called the great well because there was a sudden deep of seven hundred

fathoms where all sorts of fish congregated because of the swirl the current made against the steep walls of the floor of the ocean. Here there were concentrations of shrimp and bait fish and sometimes schools of squid in the deepest holes and these rose close to the surface at night where all the wandering fish fed on them.

In the dark the old man could feel the morning coming and as he rowed he heard the trembling sound as flying fish left the water and the hissing that their stiff set wings made as they soared away in the darkness. He was very fond of flying fish as they were his principal friends on the ocean. He was sorry for the birds, especially the small delicate dark terns that were always flying and looking and almost never finding, and he thought, "The birds have a harder life than we do except for the robber birds and the heavy strong ones. Why did they make birds so delicate and fine as those sea swallows when the ocean can be so cruel? She is kind and very beautiful. But she can be so cruel and it comes so suddenly and such birds that fly, dipping and hunting, with their small sad voices are made too delicately for the sea."

He always thought of the sea as la mar which is what people call her in Spanish when they love her. Sometimes those who love her say bad things of her but they are always said as though she were a woman. Some of the younger fishermen, those who used buoys as floats for their lines and had motorboats, bought when the shark livers had brought

much money, spoke of her as el mar which is masculine. They spoke of her as a contestant or a place or even an enemy. But the old man always thought of her as feminine and as something that gave or withheld great favours, and if she did wild or wicked things it was because she could not help them. The moon affects her as it does a woman, he thought.

He was rowing steadily and it was no effort for him since he kept well within his speed and the surface of the ocean was flat except for the occasional swirls of the current. He was letting the current do a third of the work and as it started to be light he saw he was already further out than he had hoped to be at this hour.

I worked the deep wells for a week and did nothing, he thought. Today I'll work out where the schools of bonita and albacore are and maybe there will be a big one with them.

Before it was really light he had his baits out and was drifting with the current. One bait was down forty fathoms. The second was at seventy-five and the third and fourth were down in the blue water at one hundred and one hundred and twenty-five fathoms. Each bait hung head down with the shank of the hook inside the bait fish, tied and sewed solid and all the projecting part of the hook, the curve and the point, was covered with fresh sardines. Each sardine was hooked through both eyes so that they made a half-garland on the projecting steel. There was no part of the hook that a great fish could feel which was not sweet smelling and good tasting.

The boy had given him two fresh small tunas, or albacores, which hung on the two deepest lines like plummets and, on the others, he had a big blue runner and a yellow jack that had been used before; but they were in good condition still and had the excellent sardines to give them scent and attractiveness. Each line, as thick around as a big pencil, was looped onto a green-sapped stick so that any pull or touch on the bait would make the stick dip and each line had two forty-fathom coils which could be made fast to the other spare coils so that, if it were necessary, a fish could take out over three hundred fathoms of line.

Now the man watched the dip of the three sticks over the side of the skiff and rowed gently to keep the lines straight up and down and at their proper depths. It was quite light and any moment now the sun would rise.

The sun rose thinly from the sea and the old man could see the other boats, low on the water and well in toward the shore, spread out across the current. Then the sun was brighter and the glare came on the water and then, as it rose clear, the flat sea sent it back at his eyes so that it hurt sharply and he rowed without looking into it. He looked down into the water and watched the lines that went straight down into the dark of the water. He kept them straighter than anyone did, so that at each level in the darkness of the stream there would be a bait waiting exactly where he wished it to be for any fish that swam there. Others let them drift with the

current and sometimes they were at sixty fathoms when the fishermen thought they were at a hundred.

But, he thought, I keep them with precision. Only I have no luck any more. But who knows? Maybe today. Every day is a new day. It is better to be lucky. But I would rather be exact. Then when luck comes you are ready.

The sun was two hours higher now and it did not hurt his eyes so much to look into the east. There were only three boats in sight now and they showed very low and far inshore.

All my life the early sun has hurt my eyes, he thought. Yet they are still good. In the evening I can look straight into it without getting the blackness. It has more force in the evening too. But in the morning it is painful.

Just then he saw a man-of-war bird with his long black wings circling in the sky ahead of him. He made a quick drop, slanting down on his back-swept wings, and then circled again.

"He's got something," the old man said aloud. "He's not just looking."

He rowed slowly and steadily toward where the bird was circling. He did not hurry and he kept his lines straight up and down. But he crowded the current a little so that he was still fishing correctly though faster than he would have fished if he was not trying to use the bird.

The bird went higher in the air and circled again, his wings motionless. Then he dove suddenly and the old man

saw flying fish spurt out of the water and sail desperately over the surface.

"Dolphin," the old man said aloud. "Big dolphin."

He shipped his oars and brought a small line from under the bow. It had a wire leader and a medium-sized hook and he baited it with one of the sardines. He let it go over the side and then made it fast to a ring bolt in the stern. Then he baited another line and left it coiled in the shade of the bow. He went back to rowing and to watching the long-winged black bird who was working, now, low over the water.

As he watched the bird dipped again slanting his wings for the dive and then swinging them wildly and ineffectually

as he followed the flying fish. The old man could see the slight bulge in the water that the big dolphin raised as they followed the escaping fish. The dolphin were cutting through the water below the flight of the fish and would be in the water, driving at speed, when the fish dropped. It is a big school of dolphin, he thought. They are wide spread and the flying fish have little chance. The bird has no chance. The flying fish are too big for him and they go too fast.

He watched the flying fish burst out again and again and the ineffectual movements of the bird. That school has gotten away from me, he thought. They are moving out too fast and too far. But perhaps I will pick up a stray and perhaps my big fish is around them. My big fish must be somewhere.

The clouds over the land now rose like mountains and the coast was only a long green line with the gray blue hills behind it. The water was a dark blue now, so dark that it was almost purple. As he looked down into it he saw the red sifting of the plankton in the dark water and the strange light the sun made now. He watched his lines to see them go straight down out of sight into the water and he was happy to

see so much plankton because it meant fish. The strange light the sun made in the water, now that the sun was higher, meant good weather and so did the shape of the clouds over the land. But the bird was almost out of sight now and nothing showed on the surface of the water but some patches of yellow, sun-bleached Sargasso weed and the purple, formalized, iridescent, gelatinous bladder of a Portuguese man-of-war floating close beside the boat. It turned on its side and then righted itself. It floated cheerfully as a bubble with its long deadly purple filaments trailing a yard behind it in the water.

"Agua mala," the man said. "You whore."

From where he swung lightly against his oars he looked down into the water and saw the tiny fish that were coloured like the trailing filaments and swam between them and under the small shade the bubble made as it drifted. They were immune to its poison. But men were not and when some of the filaments would catch on a line and rest there slimy and purple while the old man was working a fish, he would have welts and sores on his arms and hands of the sort that poison ivy or poison oak can give. But these poisonings from the agua mala came quickly and struck like a whiplash.

The iridescent bubbles were beautiful. But they were the falsest thing in the sea and the old man loved to see the big sea turtles eating them. The turtles saw them, approached them from the front, then shut their eyes so they were

completely carapaced and ate them filaments and all. The old man loved to see the turtles eat them and he loved to walk on them on the beach after a storm and hear them pop when he stepped on them with the horny soles of his feet.

He loved green turtles and hawks-bills with their elegance and speed and their great value and he had a friendly contempt for the huge, stupid loggerheads, yellow in their armour-plating, strange in their love-making, and happily eating the Portuguese men-of-war with their eyes shut.

He had no mysticism about turtles although he had gone in turtle boats for many years. He was sorry for them all, even the great trunk backs that were as long as the skiff and weighed a ton. Most people are heartless about turtles because a turtle's heart will beat for hours after he has been cut up and butchered. But the old man thought, I have such a heart too and my feet and hands are like theirs. He ate the white eggs to give himself strength. He ate them all through May to be strong in September and October for the truly big fish.

He also drank a cup of shark liver oil each day from the big drum in the shack where many of the fishermen kept their gear. It was there for all fishermen who wanted it. Most fishermen hated the taste. But it was no worse than getting up at the hours that they rose and it was very good against all colds and grippes and it was good for the eyes.

Now the old man looked up and saw that the bird was circling again.

"He's found fish," he said aloud. No flying fish broke the surface and there was no scattering of bait fish. But as the old man watched, a small tuna rose in the air, turned and dropped head first into the water. The tuna shone silver in the sun and after he had dropped back into the water another and another rose and they were jumping in all directions, churning the water and leaping in long jumps after the bait. They were circling it and driving it.

If they don't travel too fast I will get into them, the old man thought, and he watched the school working the water white and the bird now dropping and dipping into the bait fish that were forced to the surface in their panic.

"The bird is a great help," the old man said. Just then the stern line came taut under his foot, where he had kept a loop of the line, and he dropped his oars and felt the weight of the small tuna's shivering pull as he held the line firm and commenced to haul it in. The shivering increased as he pulled in and he could see the blue back of the fish in the water and the gold of his sides before he swung him over the side and into the boat. He lay in the stern in the sun, compact and bullet shaped, his big, unintelligent eyes staring as he thumped his life out against the planking of the boat with the quick shivering strokes of his neat, fast-moving tail. The old man hit him on the head for kindness and kicked him, his body still shuddering, under the shade of the stern.

"Albacore," he said aloud. "He'll make a beautiful bait.

He'll weigh ten pounds."

He did not remember when he had first started to talk aloud when he was by himself. He had sung when he was by himself in the old days and he had sung at night sometimes when he was alone steering on his watch in the smacks or in the turtle boats. He had probably started to talk aloud, when alone, when the boy had left. But he did not remember. When he and the boy fished together they usually spoke only when it was necessary. They talked at night or when they were storm-bound by bad weather. It was considered a virtue not to talk unnecessarily at sea and the old man had always considered it so and respected it. But now he said his thoughts aloud many times since there was no one that they could annoy.

"If the others heard me talking out loud they would think that I am crazy," he said aloud. "But since I am not crazy, I do not care. And the rich have radios to talk to them in their boats and to bring them the baseball."

Now is no time to think of baseball, he thought. Now is the time to think of only one thing. That which I was born for. There might be a big one around that school, he thought. I picked up only a straggler from the albacore that were feeding. But they are working far out and fast. Everything that shows on the surface today travels very fast and to the northeast. Can that be the time of day? Or is it some sign of weather that I do not know?

He could not see the green of the shore now but only
the tops of the blue hills that showed white as though they
were snow-capped and the clouds that looked like high snow
mountains above them. The sea was very dark and the light
made prisms in the water. The myriad flecks of the plankton
were annulled now by the high sun and it was only the great
deep prisms in the blue water that the old man saw now with
his lines going straight down into the water that was a mile
deep.

The tuna, the fishermen called all the fish of that species
tuna and only distinguished among them by their proper
names when they came to sell them or to trade them for baits,
were down again. The sun was hot now and the old man felt
it on the back of his neck and felt the sweat trickle down his
back as he rowed.

I could just drift, he thought, and sleep and put a bight
of line around my toe to wake me. But today is eighty-five
days and I should fish the day well.

Just then, watching his lines, he saw one of the projecting
green sticks dip sharply.

"Yes," he said. "Yes," and shipped his oars without
bumping the boat. He reached out for the line and held it
softly between the thumb and forefinger of his right hand.
He felt no strain nor weight and he held the line lightly. Then
it came again. This time it was a tentative pull, not solid nor
heavy, and he knew exactly what it was. One hundred fathoms

down a marlin was eating the sardines that covered the point and the shank of the hook where the hand-forged hook projected from the head of the small tuna.

The old man held the line delicately, and softly, with his left hand, unleashed it from the stick. Now he could let it run through his fingers without the fish feeling any tension.

This far out, he must be huge in this month, he thought. Eat them, fish. Eat them. Please eat them. How fresh they are and you down there six hundred feet in that cold water in the dark. Make another turn in the dark and come back and eat them.

He felt the light delicate pulling and then a harder pull when a sardine's head must have been more difficult to break from the hook. Then there was nothing.

"Come on," the old man said aloud. "Make another turn. Just smell them. Aren't they lovely? Eat them good now and then there is the tuna. Hard and cold and lovely. Don't be shy, fish. Eat them."

He waited with the line between his thumb and his finger, watching it and the other lines at the same time for the fish might have swum up or down. Then came the same delicate pulling touch again.

"He'll take it," the old man said aloud. "God help him to take it."

He did not take it though. He was gone and the old man felt nothing.

"He can't have gone," he said. "Christ knows he can't have gone. He's making a turn. Maybe he has been hooked before and he remembers something of it."

Then he felt the gentle touch on the line and he was happy.

"It was only his turn," he said. "He'll take it."

He was happy feeling the gentle pulling and then he felt something hard and unbelievably heavy. It was the weight of the fish and he let the line slip down, down, down, unrolling off the first of the two reserve coils. As it went down, slipping lightly through the old man's fingers, he still could

feel the great weight, though the pressure of his thumb and finger were almost imperceptible.

"What a fish," he said. "He has it sideways in his mouth now and he is moving off with it."

Then he will turn and swallow it, he thought. He did not say that because he knew that if you said a good thing it might not happen. He knew what a huge fish this was and he thought of him moving away in the darkness with the tuna held crosswise in his mouth. At that moment he felt him stop moving but the weight was still there. Then the weight increased and he gave more line. He tightened the pressure of his thumb and finger for a moment and the weight increased and was going straight down.

"He's taken it," he said. "Now I'll let him eat it well."

He let the line slip through his fingers while he reached down with his left hand and made fast the free end of the two reserve coils to the loop of the two reserve coils of the next line. Now he was ready. He had three forty-fathom coils of line in reserve now, as well as the coil he was using.

"Eat it a little more," he said. "Eat it well."

Eat it so that the point of the hook goes into your heart and kills you, he thought. Come up easy and let me put the harpoon into you. All right. Are you ready? Have you been long enough at table?

"Now!" he said aloud and struck hard with both hands, gained a yard of line and then struck again and again,

swinging with each arm alternately on the cord with all the strength of his arms and the pivoted weight of his body.

Nothing happened. The fish just moved away slowly and the old man could not raise him an inch. His line was strong and made for heavy fish and he held it against his back until it was so taut that beads of water were jumping from it. Then it began to make a slow hissing sound in the water and he still held it, bracing himself against the thwart and leaning back against the pull. The boat began to move slowly off toward the North-West.

The fish moved steadily and they travelled slowly on the calm water. The other baits were still in the water but there was nothing to be done.

"I wish I had the boy," the old man said aloud. "I'm being towed by a fish and I'm the towing bitt. I could make the line fast. But then he could break it. I must hold him all I can and give him line when he must have it. Thank God he is travelling and not going down."

What I will do if he decides to go down, I don't know. What I'll do if he sounds and dies I don't know. But I'll do something. There are plenty of things I can do.

He held the line against his back and watched its slant in the water and the skiff moving steadily to the North-West.

This will kill him, the old man thought. He can't do this forever. But four hours later the fish was still swimming steadily out to sea, towing the skiff, and the old man was still

braced solidly with the line across his back.

"It was noon when I hooked him," he said. "And I have never seen him."

He had pushed his straw hat hard down on his head before he hooked the fish and it was cutting his forehead. He was thirsty too and he got down on his knees and, being careful not to jerk on the line, moved as far into the bow as he could get and reached the water bottle with one hand. He opened it and drank a little. Then he rested against the bow. He rested sitting on the un-stepped mast and sail and tried not to think but only to endure.

Then he looked behind him and saw that no land was visible. That makes no difference, he thought. I can always come in on the glow from Havana. There are two more hours before the sun sets and maybe he will come up before that. If he doesn't maybe he will come up with the moon. If he does not do that maybe he will come up with the sunrise. I have no cramps and I feel strong. It is he that has the hook in his mouth. But what a fish to pull like that. He must have his mouth shut tight on the wire. I wish I could see him. I wish I could see him only once to know what I have against me.

The fish never changed his course nor his direction all that night as far as the man could tell from watching the stars. It was cold after the sun went down and the old man's sweat dried cold on his back and his arms and his old legs. During the day he had taken the sack that covered the bait box and

spread it in the sun to dry. After the sun went down he tied it around his neck so that it hung down over his back and he cautiously worked it down under the line that was across his shoulders now. The sack cushioned the line and he had found a way of leaning forward against the bow so that he was almost comfortable. The position actually was only somewhat less intolerable; but he thought of it as almost comfortable.

I can do nothing with him and he can do nothing with me, he thought. Not as long as he keeps this up.

Once he stood up and urinated over the side of the skiff and looked at the stars and checked his course. The line showed like a phosphorescent streak in the water straight out from his shoulders. They were moving more slowly now and the glow of Havana was not so strong, so that he knew the current must be carrying them to the eastward. If I lose the glare of Havana we must be going more to the eastward, he thought. For if the fish's course held true I must see it for many more hours. I wonder how the baseball came out in the grand leagues today, he thought. It would be wonderful to do this with a radio. Then he thought, think of it always. Think of what you are doing. You must do nothing stupid.

Then he said aloud, "I wish I had the boy. To help me and to see this."

No one should be alone in their old age, he thought. But it is unavoidable. I must remember to eat the tuna before he spoils in order to keep strong. Remember, no matter how

little you want to, that you must eat him in the morning. Remember, he said to himself.

During the night two porpoise came around the boat and he could hear them rolling and blowing. He could tell the difference between the blowing noise the male made and the sighing blow of the female.

"They are good," he said. "They play and make jokes and love one another. They are our brothers like the flying fish."

Then he began to pity the great fish that he had hooked. He is wonderful and strange and who knows how old he is, he thought. Never have I had such a strong fish nor one who acted so strangely. Perhaps he is too wise to jump. He could ruin me by jumping or by a wild rush. But perhaps he has been hooked many times before and he knows that this is how he should make his fight. He cannot know that it is only one man against him, nor that it is an old man. But what a great fish he is and what he will bring in the market if the flesh is good. He took the bait like a male and he pulls like a male and his fight has no panic in it. I wonder if he has any plans or if he is just as desperate as I am?

He remembered the time he had hooked one of a pair of marlin. The male fish always let the female fish feed first and the hooked fish, the female, made a wild, panic-stricken, despairing fight that soon exhausted her, and all the time the male had stayed with her, crossing the line and circling with her on the surface. He had stayed so close that the old man

老人與海

was afraid he would cut the line with his tail which was sharp as a scythe and almost of that size and shape. When the old man had gaffed her and clubbed her, holding the rapier bill with its sandpaper edge and clubbing her across the top of her head until her colour turned to a colour almost like the backing of mirrors, and then, with the boy's aid, hoisted her aboard, the male fish had stayed by the side of the boat. Then, while the old man was clearing the lines and preparing the harpoon, the male fish jumped high into the air beside the boat to see where the female was and then went down deep, his lavender wings, that were his pectoral fins, spread wide and all his wide lavender stripes showing. He was beautiful, the old man remembered, and he had stayed.

That was the saddest thing I ever saw with them, the old man thought. The boy was sad too and we begged her pardon and butchered her promptly.

"I wish the boy was here," he said aloud and settled himself against the rounded planks of the bow and felt the strength of the great fish through the line he held across his shoulders moving steadily toward whatever he had chosen.

When once, through my treachery, it had been necessary to him to make a choice, the old man thought.

His choice had been to stay in the deep dark water far out beyond all snares and traps and treacheries. My choice was to go there to find him beyond all people. Beyond all people in the world. Now we are joined together and have

been since noon. And no one to help either one of us.

Perhaps I should not have been a fisherman, he thought. But that was the thing that I was born for. I must surely remember to eat the tuna after it gets light.

Some time before daylight something took one of the baits that were behind him. He heard the stick break and the line begin to rush out over the gunwale of the skiff. In the darkness he loosened his sheath knife and taking all the strain of the fish on his left shoulder he leaned back and cut the line against the wood of the gunwale. Then he cut the other line closest to him and in the dark made the loose ends of the reserve coils fast. He worked skillfully with the one hand and put his foot on the coils to hold them as he drew his knots tight. Now he had six reserve coils of line. There were two from each bait he had severed and the two from the bait the fish had taken and they were all connected.

After it is light, he thought, I will work back to the forty-fathom bait and cut it away too and link up the reserve coils. I will have lost two hundred fathoms of good Catalan cordel and the hooks and leaders. That can be replaced. But who replaces this fish if I hook some fish and it cuts him off? I don't know what that fish was that took the bait just now. It could have been a marlin or a broadbill or a shark. I never felt him. I had to get rid of him too fast.

Aloud he said, "I wish I had the boy."

But you haven't got the boy, he thought. You have only

yourself and you had better work back to the last line now, in the dark or not in the dark, and cut it away and hook up the two reserve coils.

So he did it. It was difficult in the dark and once the fish made a surge that pulled him down on his face and made a cut below his eye. The blood ran down his cheek a little way. But it coagulated and dried before it reached his chin and he worked his way back to the bow and rested against the wood. He adjusted the sack and carefully worked the line so that it came across a new part of his shoulders and, holding it anchored with his shoulders, he carefully felt the pull of the fish and then felt with his hand the progress of the skiff through the water.

I wonder what he made that lurch for, he thought. The wire must have slipped on the great hill of his back. Certainly his back cannot feel as badly as mine does. But he cannot pull this skiff forever, no matter how great he is. Now everything is cleared away that might make trouble and I have a big reserve of line; all that a man can ask.

"Fish," he said softly, aloud, "I'll stay with you until I am dead."

He'll stay with me too, I suppose, the old man thought and he waited for it to be light. It was cold now in the time before daylight and he pushed against the wood to be warm. I can do it as long as he can, he thought. And in the first light the line extended out and down into the water. The boat

moved steadily and when the first edge of the sun rose it was on the old man's right shoulder.

"He's headed north," the old man said. The current will have set us far to the eastward, he thought. I wish he would turn with the current. That would show that he was tiring.

When the sun had risen further the old man realized that the fish was not tiring. There was only one favorable sign. The slant of the line showed he was swimming at a lesser depth. That did not necessarily mean that he would jump. But he might.

"God let him jump," the old man said. "I have enough line to handle him."

Maybe if I can increase the tension just a little it will hurt him and he will jump, he thought. Now that it is daylight let him jump so that he'll fill the sacks along his backbone with air and then he cannot go deep to die.

He tried to increase the tension, but the line had been taut up to the very edge of the breaking point since he had hooked the fish and he felt the harshness as he leaned back to pull and knew he could put no more strain on it. I must not jerk it ever, he thought. Each jerk widens the cut the hook makes and then when he does jump he might throw it. Anyway I feel better with the sun and for once I do not have to look into it.

There was yellow weed on the line but the old man knew that only made an added drag and he was pleased. It was the

老人與海

yellow Gulf weed that had made so much phosphorescence in the night.

"Fish," he said, "I love you and respect you very much. But I will kill you dead before this day ends."

Let us hope so, he thought.

A small bird came toward the skiff from the north. He was a warbler and flying very low over the water. The old man could see that he was very tired.

The bird made the stern of the boat and rested there. Then he flew around the old man's head and rested on the line where he was more comfortable.

"How old are you?" the old man asked the bird. "Is this your first trip?"

The bird looked at him when he spoke. He was too tired even to examine the line and he teetered on it as his delicate feet gripped it fast.

"It's steady," the old man told him. "It's too steady. You shouldn't be that tired after a windless night. What are birds coming to?"

The hawks, he thought, that come out to sea to meet them. But he said nothing of this to the bird who could not understand him anyway and who would learn about the hawks soon enough.

"Take a good rest, small bird," he said. "Then go in and take your chance like any man or bird or fish."

It encouraged him to talk because his back had stiffened

158

in the night and it hurt truly now.

"Stay at my house if you like, bird," he said. "I am sorry I cannot hoist the sail and take you in with the small breeze that is rising. But I am with a friend."

Just then the fish gave a sudden lurch that pulled the old man down onto the bow and would have pulled him overboard if he had not braced himself and given some line.

The bird had flown up when the line jerked and the old man had not even seen him go. He felt the line carefully with his right hand and noticed his hand was bleeding.

"Something hurt him then," he said aloud and pulled back on the line to see if he could turn the fish. But when he was touching the breaking point he held steady and settled back against the strain of the line.

"You're feeling it now, fish," he said. "And so, God knows, am I."

He looked around for the bird now because he would have liked him for company. The bird was gone.

You did not stay long, the man thought. But it is rougher where you are going until you make the shore. How did I let the fish cut me with that one quick pull he made? I must be getting very stupid. Or perhaps I was looking at the small bird and thinking of him. Now I will

pay attention to my work and then I must eat the tuna so that I will not have a failure of strength.

"I wish the boy were here and that I had some salt," he said aloud.

Shifting the weight of the line to his left shoulder and kneeling carefully he washed his hand in the ocean and held it there, submerged, for more than a minute watching the blood trail away and the steady movement of the water against his hand as the boat moved.

"He has slowed much," he said.

The old man would have liked to keep his hand in the salt water longer but he was afraid of another sudden lurch by the fish and he stood up and braced himself and held his hand up against the sun. It was only a line burn that had cut his flesh. But it was in the working part of his hand. He knew he would need his hands before this was over and he did not like to be cut before it started.

"Now," he said, when his hand had dried, "I must eat the small tuna. I can reach him with the gaff and eat him here in comfort."

He knelt down and found the tuna under the stern with the gaff and drew it toward him keeping it clear of the coiled lines. Holding the line with his left shoulder again, and bracing on his left hand and arm, he took the tuna off the gaff hook and put the gaff back in place. He put one knee on the fish and cut strips of dark red meat longitudinally from

the back of the head to the tail. They were wedge-shaped strips and he cut them from next to the back bone down to the edge of the belly. When he had cut six strips he spread them out on the wood of the bow, wiped his knife on his trousers, and lifted the carcass of the bonito by the tail and dropped it overboard.

"I don't think I can eat an entire one," he said and drew his knife across one of the strips. He could feel the steady hard pull of the line and his left hand was cramped. It drew up tight on the heavy cord and he looked at it in disgust.

"What kind of a hand is that," he said. "Cramp then if you want. Make yourself into a claw. It will do you no good."

Come on, he thought and looked down into the dark water at the slant of the line. Eat it now and it will strengthen the hand. It is not the hand's fault and you have been many hours with the fish. But you can stay with him forever. Eat the bonito now.

He picked up a piece and put it in his mouth and chewed it slowly. It was not unpleasant.

Chew it well, he thought, and get all the juices. It would not be bad to eat with a little lime or with lemon or with salt.

"How do you feel, hand?" he asked the cramped hand that was almost as stiff as rigor mortis. "I'll eat some more for you."

He ate the other part of the piece that he had cut in two. He chewed it carefully and then spat out the skin.

"How does it go, hand? Or is it too early to know?"

He took another full piece and chewed it.

"It is a strong full-blooded fish," he thought. "I was lucky to get him instead of dolphin. Dolphin is too sweet. This is hardly sweet at all and all the strength is still in it."

There is no sense in being anything but practical though, he thought. I wish I had some salt. And I do not know whether the sun will rot or dry what is left, so I had better eat it all although I am not hungry. The fish is calm and steady. I will eat it all and then I will be ready.

"Be patient, hand," he said. "I do this for you."

I wish I could feed the fish, he thought. He is my brother. But I must kill him and keep strong to do it. Slowly and conscientiously he ate all of the wedge-shaped strips of fish.

He straightened up, wiping his hand on his trousers.

"Now," he said. "You can let the cord go, hand, and I will handle him with the right arm alone until you stop that nonsense." He put his left foot on the heavy line that the left hand had held and lay back against the pull against his back.

"God help me to have the cramp go," he said. "Because I do not know what the fish is going to do."

But he seems calm, he thought, and following his plan. But what is his plan, he thought. And what is mine? Mine I must improvise to his because of his great size. If he will jump I can kill him. But he stays down forever. Then I will

stay down with him forever.

He rubbed the cramped hand against his trousers and tried to gentle the fingers. But it would not open. Maybe it will open with the sun, he thought. Maybe it will open when the strong raw tuna is digested. If I have to have it, I will open it, cost whatever it costs. But I do not want to open it now by force. Let it open by itself and come back of its own accord. After all I abused it much in the night when it was necessary to free and unite the various lines.

He looked across the sea and knew how alone he was now. But he could see the prisms in the deep dark water and the line stretching ahead and the strange undulation of the calm. The clouds were building up now for the trade wind and he looked ahead and saw a flight of wild ducks etching themselves against the sky over the water, then blurring, then etching again and he knew no man was ever alone on the sea.

He thought of how some men feared being out of sight of land in a small boat and knew they were right in the months of sudden bad weather. But now they were in hurricane months and, when there are no hurricanes, the weather of hurricane months is the best of all the year.

If there is a hurricane you always see the signs of it in the sky for days ahead, if you are at sea. They do not see it ashore because they do not know what to look for, he thought. The land must make a difference too, in the shape of the clouds. But we have no hurricane coming now.

He looked at the sky and saw the white cumulus built like friendly piles of ice cream and high above were the thin feathers of the cirrus against the high September sky.

"Light brisa," he said. "Better weather for me than for you, fish."

His left hand was still cramped, but he was unknotting it slowly.

I hate a cramp, he thought. It is a treachery of one's own body. It is humiliating before others to have a diarrhoea from ptomaine poisoning or to vomit from it. But a cramp, he thought of it as a calambre, humiliates oneself especially when one is alone.

If the boy were here he could rub it for me and loosen it down from the forearm, he thought. But it will loosen up.

Then, with his right hand he felt the difference in the pull of the line before he saw the slant change in the water. Then, as he leaned against the line and slapped his left hand hard and fast against his thigh he saw the line slanting slowly upward.

"He's coming up," he said. "Come on hand. Please come on."

The line rose slowly and steadily and then the surface of the ocean bulged ahead of the boat and the fish came out. He came out unendingly and water poured from his sides. He was bright in the sun and his head and back were dark purple and in the sun the stripes on his sides showed wide and a light

lavender. His sword was as long as a baseball bat and tapered like a rapier and he rose his full length from the water and then re-entered it, smoothly, like a diver and the old man saw the great scythe-blade of his tail go under and the line commenced to race out.

"He is two feet longer than the skiff," the old man said. The line was going out fast but steadily and the fish was not panicked. The old man was trying with both hands to keep the line just inside of breaking strength. He knew that if he could not slow the fish with a steady pressure the fish could take out all the line and break it.

He is a great fish and I must convince him, he thought. I must never let him learn his strength nor what he could do if he made his run. If I were him I would put in everything now and go until something broke. But, thank God, they are not as intelligent as we who kill them; although they are more noble and more able.

The old man had seen many great fish. He had seen many that weighed more than a thousand pounds and he had caught two of that size in his life, but never alone. Now alone, and out of sight of land, he was fast to the biggest fish that he had ever seen and bigger than he had ever heard of, and his left hand was still as tight as the gripped claws of an eagle.

It will uncramp though, he thought. Surely it will uncramp to help my right hand. There are three things that are brothers: the fish and my two hands. It must uncramp. It

is unworthy of it to be cramped. The fish had slowed again and was going at his usual pace.

I wonder why he jumped, the old man thought. He jumped almost as though to show me how big he was. I know now, anyway, he thought. I wish I could show him what sort of man I am. But then he would see the cramped hand. Let him think I am more man than I am and I will be so. I wish I was the fish, he thought, with everything he has against only my will and my intelligence.

He settled comfortably against the wood and took his suffering as it came and the fish swam steadily and the boat moved slowly through the dark water. There was a small sea rising with the wind coming up from the east and at noon the old man's left hand was uncramped.

"Bad news for you, fish," he said and shifted the line over the sacks that covered his shoulders.

He was comfortable but suffering, although he did not admit the suffering at all.

"I am not religious," he said. "But I will say ten Our Fathers and ten Hail Marys that I should catch this fish, and I promise to make a pilgrimage to the Virgen de Cobre if I catch him. That is a promise."

He commenced to say his prayers mechanically. Sometimes he would be so tired that he could not remember the prayer and then he would say them fast so that they would come automatically. Hail Marys are easier to say than Our

Fathers, he thought.

"Hail Mary full of Grace the Lord is with thee. Blessed art thou among women and blessed is the fruit of thy womb, Jesus. Holy Mary, Mother of God, pray for us sinners now and at the hour of our death. Amen." Then he added, "Blessed Virgin, pray for the death of this fish. Wonderful though he is."

With his prayers said, and feeling much better, but suffering exactly as much, and perhaps a little more, he leaned against the wood of the bow and began, mechanically, to work the fingers of his left hand.

The sun was hot now although the breeze was rising gently.

"I had better re-bait that little line out over the stern," he said. "If the fish decides to stay another night I will need to eat again and the water is low in the bottle. I don't think I can get anything but a dolphin here. But if I eat him fresh enough he won't be bad. I wish a flying fish would come on board tonight. But I have no light to attract them. A flying fish is excellent to eat raw and I would not have to cut him up. I must save all my strength now. Christ, I did not know he was so big."

"I'll kill him though," he said. "In all his greatness and his glory."

Although it is unjust, he thought. But I will show him

what a man can do and what a man endures.

"I told the boy I was a strange old man," he said. "Now is when I must prove it."

The thousand times that he had proved it meant nothing. Now he was proving it again. Each time was a new time and he never thought about the past when he was doing it.

I wish he'd sleep and I could sleep and dream about the lions, he thought. Why are the lions the main thing that is left? Don't think, old man, he said to himself. Rest gently now against the wood and think of nothing. He is working. Work as little as you can.

It was getting into the afternoon and the boat still moved slowly and steadily. But there was an added drag now from the easterly breeze and the old man rode gently with the small sea and the hurt of the cord across his back came to him easily and smoothly.

Once in the afternoon the line started to rise again. But the fish only continued to swim at a slightly higher level. The sun was on the old man's left arm and shoulder and on his back. So he knew the fish had turned east of north.

Now that he had seen him once, he could picture the fish swimming in the water with his purple pectoral fins set wide as wings and the great erect tail slicing through the dark. I wonder how much he sees at that depth, the old man thought. His eye is huge and a horse, with much less eye, can see in the dark. Once I could see quite well in the dark. Not in the

absolute dark. But almost as a cat sees.

The sun and his steady movement of his fingers had uncramped his left hand now completely and he began to shift more of the strain to it and he shrugged the muscles of his back to shift the hurt of the cord a little.

"If you're not tired, fish," he said aloud, "you must be very strange."

He felt very tired now and he knew the night would come soon and he tried to think of other things. He thought of the Big Leagues, to him they were the Gran Ligas, and he knew that the Yankees of New York were playing the Tigres of Detroit.

This is the second day now that I do not know the result of the juegos, he thought. But I must have confidence and I must be worthy of the great DiMaggio who does all things perfectly even with the pain of the bone spur in his heel. What is a bone spur? he asked himself. Un espuela de hueso. We do not have them. Can it be as painful as the spur of a fighting cock in one's heel? I do not think I could endure that or the loss of the eye and of both eyes and continue to fight as the fighting cocks do. Man is not much beside the great birds and beasts. Still I would rather be that beast down there in the darkness of the sea.

"Unless sharks come," he said aloud. "If sharks come, God pity him and me."

Do you believe the great DiMaggio would stay with a fish

as long as I will stay with this one? he thought. I am sure he would and more since he is young and strong. Also his father was a fisherman. But would the bone spur hurt him too much?

"I do not know," he said aloud. "I never had a bone spur."

As the sun set he remembered, to give himself more confidence, the time in the tavern at Casablanca when he had played the hand game with the great negro from Cienfuegos who was the strongest man on the docks. They had gone one day and one night with their elbows on a chalk line on the table and their forearms straight up and their hands gripped tight. Each one was trying to force the other's hand down onto the table. There was much betting and people went in and out of the room under the kerosene lights and he had looked at the arm and hand of the negro and at the negro's face. They changed the referees every four hours after the first eight so that the referees

could sleep. Blood came out from under the fingernails of both his and the negro's hands and they looked each other in the eye and at their hands and forearms and the bettors went in and out of the room and sat on high chairs against the wall and watched. The walls were painted bright blue and were of wood and the lamps threw their shadows against them. The negro's shadow was huge and it moved on the wall as the breeze moved the lamps.

The odds would change back and forth all night and they fed the negro rum and lighted cigarettes for him.

Then the negro, after the rum, would try for a tremendous effort and once he had the old man, who was not an old man then but was Santiago El Campeon, nearly three inches off balance. But the old man had raised his hand up to dead even again. He was sure then that he had the negro, who was a fine man and a great athlete, beaten. And at daylight when the bettors were asking that it be called a draw and the referee was shaking his head, he had unleashed his effort and forced the hand of the negro down and down until it rested on the wood.

The match had started on a Sunday morning and ended on a Monday morning. Many of the bettors had asked for a draw because they had to go to work on the docks loading sacks of sugar or at the Havana Coal Company. Otherwise everyone would have wanted it to go to a finish. But he had finished it anyway and before anyone had to go to work.

For a long time after that everyone had called him The Champion and there had been a return match in the spring. But not much money was bet and he had won it quite easily since he had broken the confidence of the negro from Cienfuegos in the first match. After that he had a few matches and then no more. He decided that he could beat anyone if he wanted to badly enough and he decided that it was bad for his right hand for fishing. He had tried a few practice matches with his left hand. But his left hand had always been a traitor and would not do what he called on it to do and he did not trust it.

The sun will bake it out well now, he thought. It should not cramp on me again unless it gets too cold in the night. I wonder what this night will bring.

An airplane passed over head on its course to Miami and he watched its shadow scaring up the schools of flying fish.

"With so much flying fish there should be dolphin," he said, and leaned back on the line to see if it was possible to gain any on his fish. But he could not and it stayed at the hardness and water-drop shivering that preceded breaking. The boat moved ahead slowly and he watched the airplane until he could no longer see it.

It must be very strange in an airplane, he thought. I wonder what the sea looks like from that height? They should be able to see the fish well if they do not fly too high. I would like to fly very slowly at two hundred fathoms high and see

the fish from above. In the turtle boats I was in the cross-trees of the mast-head and even at that height I saw much. The dolphin look greener from there and you can see their stripes and their purple spots and you can see all of the school as they swim. Why is it that all the fast-moving fish of the dark current have purple backs and usually purple stripes or spots? The dolphin looks green of course because he is really golden. But when he comes to feed, truly hungry, purple stripes show on his sides as on a marlin. Can it be anger, or the greater speed he makes that brings them out?

Just before it was dark, as they passed a great island of Sargasso weed that heaved and swung in the light sea as though the ocean were making love with something under a yellow blanket, his small line was taken by a dolphin. He saw it first when it jumped in the air, true gold in the last of the sun and bending and flapping wildly in the air. It jumped again and again in the acrobatics of its fear and he worked his way back to the stern and crouching and holding the big line with his right hand and arm, he pulled the dolphin in with his left hand, stepping on the gained line each time with his bare left foot. When the fish was at the stern, plunging and cutting from side to side in desperation, the old man leaned over the stern and lifted the burnished gold fish with its purple spots over the stern. Its jaws were working convulsively in quick bites against the hook and it pounded the bottom of the skiff with its long flat body, its tail and its head until he clubbed it

across the shining golden head until it shivered and was still.

The old man unhooked the fish, rebaited the line with another sardine and tossed it over. Then he worked his way slowly back to the bow. He washed his left hand and wiped it on his trousers. Then he shifted the heavy line from his right hand to his left and washed his right hand in the sea while he watched the sun go into the ocean and the slant of the big cord.

"He hasn't changed at all," he said. But watching the movement of the water against his hand he noted that it was perceptibly slower.

"I'll lash the two oars together across the stern and that will slow him in the night," he said. "He's good for the night and so am I."

It would be better to gut the dolphin a little later to save the blood in the meat, he thought. I can do that a little later and lash the oars to make a drag at the same time. I had better keep the fish quiet now and not disturb him too much at sunset. The setting of the sun is a difficult time for all fish.

He let his hand dry in the air then grasped the line with it and eased himself as much as he could and allowed himself to be pulled forward against the wood so that the boat took the strain as much, or more, than he did.

I'm learning how to do it, he thought. This part of it anyway. Then too, remember he hasn't eaten since he took the bait and he is huge and needs much food. I have eaten the

whole bonito. Tomorrow I will eat the dolphin. He called it dorado. Perhaps I should eat some of it when I clean it. It will be harder to eat than the bonito. But, then, nothing is easy.

"How do you feel, fish?" he asked aloud. "I feel good and my left hand is better and I have food for a night and a day. Pull the boat, fish."

He did not truly feel good because the pain from the cord across his back had almost passed pain and gone into a dullness that he mistrusted. But I have had worse things than that, he thought. My hand is only cut a little and the cramp is gone from the other. My legs are all right. Also now I have gained on him in the question of sustenance.

It was dark now as it becomes dark quickly after the sun sets in September. He lay against the worn wood of the bow and rested all that he could. The first stars were out. He did not know the name of Rigel but he saw it and knew soon they would all be out and he would have all his distant friends.

"The fish is my friend too," he said aloud. "I have never seen or heard of such a fish. But I must kill him. I am glad we do not have to try to kill the stars."

Imagine if each day a man must try to kill the moon, he thought. The moon runs away. But imagine if a man each day should have to try to kill the sun? We were born lucky, he thought.

Then he was sorry for the great fish that had nothing to eat and his determination to kill him never relaxed in his

sorrow for him. How many people will he feed, he thought. But are they worthy to eat him? No, of course not. There is no one worthy of eating him from the manner of his behaviour and his great dignity.

I do not understand these things, he thought. But it is good that we do not have to try to kill the sun or the moon or the stars. It is enough to live on the sea and kill our true brothers.

Now, he thought, I must think about the drag. It has its perils and its merits. I may lose so much line that I will lose him, if he makes his effort and the drag made by the oars is in place and the boat loses all her lightness. Her lightness prolongs both our suffering but it is my safety since he has great speed that he has never yet employed. No matter what passes I must gut the dolphin so he does not spoil and eat some of him to be strong.

Now I will rest an hour more and feel that he is solid and steady before I move back to the stern to do the work and make the decision. In the meantime I can see how he acts and if he shows any changes. The oars are a good trick; but it has reached the time to play for safety. He is much fish still and I saw that the hook was in the corner of his mouth and he has kept his mouth tight shut. The punishment of the hook is nothing. The punishment of hunger, and that he is against something that he does not comprehend, is everything. Rest now, old man, and let him work until your next duty comes.

He rested for what he believed to be two hours. The moon did not rise now until late and he had no way of judging the time. Nor was he really resting except comparatively. He was still bearing the pull of the fish across his shoulders but he placed his left hand on the gunwale of the bow and confided more and more of the resistance to the fish to the skiff itself.

How simple it would be if I could make the line fast, he thought. But with one small lurch he could break it. I must cushion the pull of the line with my body and at all times be ready to give line with both hands.

"But you have not slept yet, old man," he said aloud. "It is half a day and a night and now another day and you have not slept. You must devise a way so that you sleep a little if he is quiet and steady. If you do not sleep you might become unclear in the head."

I'm clear enough in the head, he thought. Too clear. I am as clear as the stars that are my brothers. Still I must sleep. They sleep and the moon and the sun sleep and even the ocean sleeps sometimes on certain days when there is no current and a flat calm.

But remember to sleep, he thought. Make yourself do it and devise some simple and sure way about the lines. Now go back and prepare the dolphin. It is too dangerous to rig the oars as a drag if you must sleep.

老人與海

I could go without sleeping, he told himself. But it would be too dangerous.

He started to work his way back to the stern on his hands and knees, being careful not to jerk against the fish. He may be half asleep himself, he thought. But I do not want him to rest. He must pull until he dies.

Back in the stern he turned so that his left hand held the strain of the line across his shoulders and drew his knife from its sheath with his right hand. The stars were bright now and he saw the dolphin clearly and he pushed the blade of his knife into his head and drew him out from under the stern. He put one of his feet on the fish and slit him quickly from the vent up to the tip of his lower jaw. Then he put his knife down and gutted him with his right hand, scooping him clean and pulling the gills clear.

He felt the maw heavy and slippery in his hands and he slit it open. There were two flying fish inside. They were fresh and hard and he laid them side by side and dropped the guts and the gills over the stern. They sank leaving a trail of phosphorescence in the water. The dolphin was cold and a leprous gray-white now in the starlight and the old man skinned one side of him while he held his right foot on the fish's head. Then he turned him over and skinned the other side and cut each side off from the head down to the tail.

He slid the carcass overboard and looked to see if there was any swirl in the water. But there was only the light of its

slow descent. He turned then and placed the two flying fish inside the two fillets of fish and putting his knife back in its sheath, he worked his way slowly back to the bow. His back was bent with the weight of the line across it and he carried the fish in his right hand.

Back in the bow he laid the two fillets of fish out on the wood with the flying fish beside them. After that he settled the line across his shoulders in a new place and held it again with his left hand resting on the gunwale. Then he leaned over the side and washed the flying fish in the water, noting the speed of the water against his hand. His hand was phosphorescent from skinning the fish and he watched the flow of the water against it. The flow was less strong and as he rubbed the side of his hand against the planking of the skiff, particles of phosphorus floated off and drifted slowly astern.

"He is tiring or he is resting," the old man said. "Now let me get through the eating of this dolphin and get some rest and a little sleep."

Under the stars and with the night colder all the time he ate half of one of the dolphin fillets and one of the flying fish, gutted and with its head cut off.

"What an excellent fish dolphin is to eat cooked," he said. "And what a miserable fish raw. I will never go in a boat again without salt or limes."

If I had brains I would have splashed water on the bow

all day and drying, it would have made salt, he thought. But then I did not hook the dolphin until almost sunset. Still it was a lack of preparation. But I have chewed it all well and I am not nauseated.

The sky was clouding over to the east and one after another the stars he knew were gone. It looked now as though he were moving into a great canyon of clouds and the wind had dropped.

"There will be bad weather in three or four days," he said. "But not tonight and not tomorrow. Rig now to get some sleep, old man, while the fish is calm and steady."

He held the line tight in his right hand and then pushed his thigh against his right hand as he leaned all his weight against the wood of the bow. Then he passed the line a little lower on his shoulders and braced his left hand on it.

My right hand can hold it as long as it is braced, he thought. If it relaxes in sleep my left hand will wake me as the line goes out. It is hard on the right hand. But he is used to punishment. Even if I sleep twenty minutes or a half an hour it is good. He lay forward cramping himself against the line with all of his body, putting all his weight onto his right hand, and he was asleep.

He did not dream of the lions but instead of a vast school of porpoises that stretched for eight or ten miles and it was in the time of their mating and they would leap high

into the air and return into the same hole they had made in the water when they leaped.

Then he dreamed that he was in the village on his bed and there was a norther and he was very cold and his right arm was asleep because his head had rested on it instead of a pillow.

After that he began to dream of the long yellow beach and he saw the first of the lions come down onto it in the early dark and then the other lions came and he rested his chin on the wood of the bows where the ship lay anchored with the evening off-shore breeze and he waited to see if there would be more lions and he was happy.

The moon had been up for a long time but he slept on and the fish pulled on steadily and the boat moved into the tunnel of clouds.

He woke with the jerk of his right fist coming up against his face and the line burning out through his right hand. He had no feeling of his left hand but he braked all he could with his right and the line rushed out. Finally his left hand found the line and he leaned back against the line and now it burned his back and his left hand, and his left hand was taking all the strain and cutting badly. He looked back at the coils of line and they were feeding smoothly. Just then the fish jumped making a great bursting of the ocean and then a heavy fall. Then he jumped again and again and the boat was going fast although line was still racing out and the old man was raising

the strain to breaking point and raising it to breaking point
again and again. He had been pulled down tight onto the bow
and his face was in the cut slice of dolphin and he could not
move.

This is what we waited for, he thought. So now let us
take it.

Make him pay for the line, he thought. Make him pay for
it.

He could not see the fish's jumps but only heard the
breaking of the ocean and the heavy splash as he fell. The
speed of the line was cutting his hands badly but he had
always known this would happen and he tried to keep the
cutting across the calloused parts and not let the line slip into

the palm nor cut the fingers.

If the boy was here he would wet the coils of line, he thought. Yes. If the boy were here. If the boy were here.

The line went out and out and out but it was slowing now and he was making the fish earn each inch of it. Now he got his head up from the wood and out of the slice of fish that his cheek had crushed. Then he was on his knees and then he rose slowly to his feet. He was ceding line but more slowly all the time. He worked back to where he could feel with his foot the coils of line that he could not see. There was plenty of line still and now the fish had to pull the friction of all that new line through the water.

Yes, he thought. And now he has jumped more than a dozen times and filled the sacks along his back with air and he cannot go down deep to die where I cannot bring him up. He will start circling soon and then I must work on him. I wonder what started him so suddenly? Could it have been hunger that made him desperate, or was he frightened by something in the night? Maybe he suddenly felt fear. But he was such a calm, strong fish and he seemed so fearless and so confident. It is strange.

"You better be fearless and confident yourself, old man," he said. "You're holding him again but you cannot get line. But soon he has to circle."

The old man held him with his left hand and his shoulders now and stooped down and scooped up water in

his right hand to get the crushed dolphin flesh off of his face. He was afraid that it might nauseate him and he would vomit and lose his strength. When his face was cleaned he washed his right hand in the water over the side and then let it stay in the salt water while he watched the first light come before the sunrise. He's headed almost east, he thought. That means he is tired and going with the current. Soon he will have to circle. Then our true work begins.

After he judged that his right hand had been in the water long enough he took it out and looked at it. "It is not bad," he said. "And pain does not matter to a man."

He took hold of the line carefully so that it did not fit into any of the fresh line cuts and shifted his weight so that he could put his left hand into the sea on the other side of the skiff.

"You did not do so badly for something worthless," he said to his left hand. "But there was a moment when I could not find you."

Why was I not born with two good hands? he thought. Perhaps it was my fault in not training that one properly. But God knows he has had enough chances to learn. He did not do so badly in the night, though, and he has only cramped once. If he cramps again let the line cut him off.

When he thought that he knew that he was not being clear-headed and he thought he should chew some more of the dolphin. But I can't, he told himself. It is better to be

light-headed than to lose your strength from nausea. And I know I cannot keep it if I eat it since my face was in it. I will keep it for an emergency until it goes bad. But it is too late to try for strength now through nourishment. You're stupid, he told himself. Eat the other flying fish.

It was there, cleaned and ready, and he picked it up with his left hand and ate it chewing the bones carefully and eating all of it down to the tail.

It has more nourishment than almost any fish, he thought. At least the kind of strength that I need. Now I have done what I can, he thought. Let him begin to circle and let the fight come.

The sun was rising for the third time since he had put to sea when the fish started to circle.

He could not see by the slant of the line that the fish was circling. It was too early for that. He just felt a faint slackening of the pressure of the line and he commenced to pull on it gently with his right hand. It tightened, as always, but just when he reached the point where it would break, line began to come in. He slipped his shoulders and head from under the line and began to pull in line steadily and gently. He used both of his hands in a swinging motion and tried to do the pulling as much as he could with his body and his legs. His old legs and shoulders pivoted with the swinging of the pulling.

"It is a very big circle," he said. "But he is circling."

Then the line would not come in any more and he held it

until he saw the drops jumping from it in the sun. Then it started out and the old man knelt down and let it go grudgingly back into the dark water.

"He is making the far part of his circle now," he said. I must hold all I can, he thought. The strain will shorten his circle each time. Perhaps in an hour I will see him. Now I must convince him and then I must kill him.

But the fish kept on circling slowly and the old man was wet with sweat and tired deep into his bones two hours later. But the circles were much shorter now and from the way the line slanted he could tell the fish had risen steadily while he swam.

For an hour the old man had been seeing black spots before his eyes and the sweat salted his eyes and salted the cut over his eye and on his forehead. He was not afraid of the black spots. They were normal at the tension that he was pulling on the line. Twice, though, he had felt faint and dizzy and that had worried him.

"I could not fail myself and die on a fish like this," he said. "Now that I have him coming so beautifully, God help me endure. I'll say a hundred Our Fathers and a hundred Hail Marys. But I cannot say them now."

Consider them said, he thought. I'll say them later.

Just then he felt a sudden banging and jerking on the line he held with his two hands. It was sharp and hard-feeling and heavy.

He is hitting the wire leader with his spear, he thought. That was bound to come. He had to do that. It may make him jump though and I would rather he stayed circling now. The jumps were necessary for him to take air. But after that each one can widen the opening of the hook wound and he can throw the hook.

"Don't jump, fish," he said. "Don't jump."

The fish hit the wire several times more and each time he shook his head the old man gave up a little line.

I must hold his pain where it is, he thought. Mine does not matter. I can control mine. But his pain could drive him mad.

After a while the fish stopped beating at the wire and started circling slowly again. The old man was gaining line steadily now. But he felt faint again. He lifted some sea water with his left hand and put it on his head. Then he put more on and rubbed the back of his neck.

"I have no cramps," he said. "He'll be up soon and I can last. You have to last. Don't even speak of it."

He kneeled against the bow and, for a moment, slipped the line over his back again. I'll rest now while he goes out on the circle and then stand up and work on him when he comes in, he decided.

It was a great temptation to rest in the bow and let the fish make one circle by himself without recovering any line. But when the strain showed the fish had turned to come

toward the boat, the old man rose to his feet and started the pivoting and the weaving pulling that brought in all the line he gained.

I'm tireder than I have ever been, he thought, and now the trade wind is rising. But that will be good to take him in with. I need that badly.

"I'll rest on the next turn as he goes out," he said. "I feel much better. Then in two or three turns more I will have him."

His straw hat was far on the back of his head and he sank down into the bow with the pull of the line as he felt the fish turn.

You work now, fish, he thought. I'll take you at the turn.

The sea had risen considerably. But it was a fair-weather breeze and he had to have it to get home.

"I'll just steer south and west," he said. "A man is never lost at sea and it is a long island."

It was on the third turn that he saw the fish first.

He saw him first as a dark shadow that took so long to pass under the boat that he could not believe its length.

"No," he said. "He can't be that big."

But he was that big and at the end of this circle he came to the surface only thirty yards away and the man saw his tail out of water. It was higher than a big scythe blade and a very pale lavender above the dark blue water. It raked back and as the fish swam just below the surface the old man could see

The Old Man and the Sea

his huge bulk and the purple stripes that banded him. His dorsal fin was down and his huge pectorals were spread wide.

On this circle the old man could see the fish's eye and the two gray sucking fish that swam around him. Sometimes they attached themselves to him. Sometimes they darted off. Sometimes they would swim easily in his shadow. They were each over three feet long and when they swam fast they lashed their whole bodies like eels.

The old man was sweating now but from something else besides the sun. On each calm placid turn the fish made he was gaining line and he was sure that in two turns more he would have a chance to get the harpoon in.

But I must get him close, close, close, he thought. I mustn't try for the head. I must get the heart.

"Be calm and strong, old man," he said.

On the next circle the fish's back was out but he was a little too far from the boat.

On the next circle he was still too far away but he was higher out of water and the old man was sure that by gaining some more line he could have him alongside.

He had rigged his harpoon long before and its coil of light rope was in a round basket and the end was made fast to the bitt in the bow.

The fish was coming in on his circle now calm and beautiful looking and only his great tail moving. The old man pulled on him all that he could to bring him closer. For just a

moment the fish turned a little on his side. Then he straightened himself and began another circle.

"I moved him," the old man said. "I moved him then."

He felt faint again now but he held on the great fish all the strain that he could. I moved him, he thought. Maybe this time I can get him over. Pull, hands, he thought. Hold up, legs. Last for me, head. Last for me. You never went. This time I'll pull him over.

But when he put all of his effort on, starting it well out before the fish came alongside and pulling with all his strength, the fish pulled part way over and then righted himself and swam away.

"Fish," the old man said. "Fish, you are going to have to die anyway. Do you have to kill me too?"

That way nothing is accomplished, he thought. His mouth was too dry to speak but he could not reach for the water now. I must get him alongside this time, he thought. I am not good for many more turns. Yes you are, he told himself. You're good for ever.

On the next turn, he nearly had him. But again the fish righted himself and swam slowly away.

You are killing me, fish, the old man thought. But you have a right to. Never have I seen a greater, or more beautiful, or a calmer or more noble thing than you, brother. Come on and kill me. I do not care who kills who.

Now you are getting confused in the head, he thought.

You must keep your head clear. Keep your head clear and know how to suffer like a man. Or a fish, he thought.

"Clear up, head," he said in a voice he could hardly hear. "Clear up."

Twice more it was the same on the turns.

I do not know, the old man thought. He had been on the point of feeling himself go each time. I do not know. But I will try it once more.

He tried it once more and he felt himself going when he turned the fish. The fish righted himself and swam off again slowly with the great tail weaving in the air.

I'll try it again, the old man promised, although his hands were mushy now and he could only see well in flashes.

He tried it again and it was the same. So, he thought, and he felt himself going before he started; I will try it once again.

He took all his pain and what was left of his strength and his long gone pride and he put it against the fish's agony and the fish came over onto his side and swam gently on his side, his bill almost touching the planking of the skiff and started to pass the boat, long, deep, wide, silver and barred with purple and interminable in the water.

The old man dropped the line and put his foot on it and lifted the harpoon as high as he could and drove it down with all his strength, and more strength he had just summoned, into the fish's side just behind the great chest fin that rose high in the air to the altitude of the man's chest. He felt the

iron go in and he leaned on it and drove it further and then pushed all his weight after it.

Then the fish came alive, with his death in him, and rose high out of the water showing all his great length and width and all his power and his beauty. He seemed to hang in the air above the old man in the skiff. Then he fell into the water with a crash that sent spray over the old man and over all of the skiff.

The old man felt faint and sick and he could not see well. But he cleared the harpoon line and let it run slowly through his raw hands and, when he could see, he saw the fish was on his back with his silver belly up. The shaft of the harpoon was projecting at an angle from the fish's shoulder and the sea was discolouring with the red of the blood from his heart. First it was dark as a shoal in the blue water that was more than a mile deep. Then it spread like a cloud. The fish was silvery and still and floated with the waves.

The old man looked carefully in the glimpse of vision that he had. Then he took two turns of the harpoon line around the bitt in the bow and laid his head on his hands.

"Keep my head clear," he said against the wood of the bow. "I am a tired old man. But I have killed this fish which is my brother and now I must do the slave work."

Now I must prepare the nooses and the rope to lash him alongside, he thought. Even if we were two and swamped her to load him and bailed her out, this skiff would never hold

him. I must prepare everything, then bring him in and lash him well and step the mast and set sail for home.

He started to pull the fish in to have him alongside so that he could pass a line through his gills and out his mouth and make his head fast alongside the bow. I want to see him, he thought, and to touch and to feel him. He is my fortune, he thought. But that is not why I wish to feel him. I think I felt his heart, he thought. When I pushed on the harpoon shaft the second time. Bring him in now and make him fast and get the noose around his tail and another around his middle to bind him to the skiff.

"Get to work, old man," he said. He took a very small drink of the water. "There is very much slave work to be done now that the fight is over."

He looked up at the sky and then out to his fish. He looked at the sun carefully. It is not much more than noon, he thought. And the trade wind is rising. The lines all mean nothing now. The boy and I will splice them when we are home.

"Come on, fish," he said. But the fish did not come. Instead he lay there wallowing now in the seas and the old man pulled the skiff up onto him.

When he was even with him and had the fish's head against the bow he could not believe his size. But he untied the harpoon rope from the bitt, passed it through the fish's gills and out his jaws, made a turn around his sword then

老人與海

passed the rope through the other gill, made another turn around the bill and knotted the double rope and made it fast to the bitt in the bow. He cut the rope then and went astern to noose the tail. The fish had turned silver from his original purple and silver, and the stripes showed the same pale violet colour as his tail. They were wider than a man's hand with his fingers spread and the fish's eye looked as detached as the mirrors in a periscope or as a saint in a procession.

"It was the only way to kill him," the old man said. He was feeling better since the water and he knew he would not go away and his head was clear. He's over fifteen hundred pounds the way he is, he thought. Maybe much more. If he dresses out two-thirds of that at thirty cents a pound?

"I need a pencil for that," he said. "My head is not that clear. But I think the great DiMaggio would be proud of me today. I had no bone spurs. But the hands and the back hurt truly." I wonder what a bone spur is, he thought. Maybe we have them without knowing of it.

He made the fish fast to bow and stern and to the middle thwart. He was so big it was like lashing a much bigger skiff alongside. He cut a piece of line and tied the fish's lower jaw against his bill so his mouth would not open and they would sail as cleanly as possible. Then he stepped the mast and, with the stick that was his gaff and with his boom rigged, the patched sail drew, the boat began to move, and half lying in the stern he sailed south-west.

He did not need a compass to tell him where south-west was. He only needed the feel of the trade wind and the drawing of the sail. I better put a small line out with a spoon on it and try and get something to eat and drink for the moisture. But he could not find a spoon and his sardines were rotten. So he hooked a patch of yellow gulf weed with the gaff as they passed and shook it so that the small shrimps that were in it fell onto the planking of the skiff. There were more than a dozen of them and they jumped and kicked like sand fleas. The old man pinched their heads off with his thumb and forefinger and ate them chewing up the shells and the tails. They were very tiny but he knew they were nourishing and they tasted good.

The old man still had two drinks of water in the bottle and he used half of one after he had eaten the shrimps. The skiff was sailing well considering the handicaps and he steered with the tiller under his arm. He could see the fish and he had only to look at his hands and feel his back against the stern to know that this had truly happened and was not a dream. At one time when he was feeling so badly toward the end, he had thought perhaps it was a dream. Then when he had seen the fish come out of the water and hang motionless in the sky before he fell, he was sure there was some great strangeness and he could not believe it. Then he could not see well, although now he saw as well as ever.

Now he knew there was the fish and his hands and back

were no dream. The hands cure quickly, he thought. I bled them clean and the salt water will heal them. The dark water of the true gulf is the greatest healer that there is. All I must do is keep the head clear. The hands have done their work and we sail well. With his mouth shut and his tail straight up and down we sail like brothers. Then his head started to become a little unclear and he thought, is he bringing me in or am I bringing him in? If I were towing him behind there would be no question. Nor if the fish were in the skiff, with all dignity gone, there would be no question either. But they were sailing together lashed side by side and the old man thought, let him bring me in if it pleases him. I am only better than him through trickery and he meant me no harm.

They sailed well and the old man soaked his hands in the salt water and tried to keep his head clear. There were high cumulus clouds and enough cirrus above them so that the old man knew the breeze would last all night. The old man looked at the fish constantly to make sure it was true. It was an hour before the first shark hit him.

The shark was not an accident. He had come up from deep down in the water as the dark cloud of blood had settled and dispersed in the mile deep sea. He had come up so fast and absolutely without caution that he broke the surface of the blue water and was in the sun. Then he fell back into the sea and picked up the scent and started swimming on the course the skiff and the fish had taken.

Sometimes he lost the scent. But he would pick it up again, or have just a trace of it, and he swam fast and hard on the course. He was a very big Mako shark built to swim as fast as the fastest fish in the sea and everything about him was beautiful except his jaws.

His back was as blue as a sword fish's and his belly was silver and his hide was smooth and handsome. He was built as a sword fish except for his huge jaws which were tight shut now as he swam fast, just under the surface with his high dorsal fin knifing through the water without wavering. Inside the closed double lip of his jaws all of his eight rows of teeth were slanted inwards. They were not the ordinary pyramid-shaped teeth of most sharks. They were shaped like a man's fingers when they are crisped like claws. They were nearly as long as the fingers of the old man and they had razor-sharp cutting edges on both sides. This was a fish built to feed on all the fishes in the sea, that were so fast and strong and well armed that they had no other enemy. Now he speeded up as he smelled the fresher scent and his blue dorsal fin cut the water.

When the old man saw him coming he knew that this was a shark that had no fear at all and would do exactly what he wished. He prepared the harpoon and made the rope fast while he watched the shark come on. The rope was short as it lacked what he had cut away to lash the fish.

The old man's head was clear and good now and he was

full of resolution but he had little hope. It was too good to last, he thought. He took one look at the great fish as he watched the shark close in. It might as well have been a dream, he thought. I cannot keep him from hitting me but maybe I can get him. Dentuso, he thought. Bad luck to your mother.

The shark closed fast astern and when he hit the fish the old man saw his mouth open and his strange eyes and the clicking chop of the teeth as he drove forward in the meat just above the tail. The shark's head was out of water and his back was coming out and the old man could hear the noise of skin and flesh ripping on the big fish when he rammed the harpoon down onto the shark's head at a spot where the line between his eyes intersected with the line that ran straight back from his nose. There were no such lines. There was only the heavy sharp blue head and the big eyes and the clicking, thrusting all-swallowing jaws. But that was the location of the brain and the old man hit it. He hit it with his blood mushed hands driving a good harpoon with all his strength. He hit it without hope but with resolution and complete malignancy.

The shark swung over and the old man saw his eye was not alive and then he swung over once again, wrapping himself in two loops of the rope. The old man knew that he was dead but the shark would not accept it. Then, on his back, with his tail lashing and his jaws clicking, the shark plowed over the water as a speed-boat does. The water was

white where his tail beat it and three-quarters of his body was clear above the water when the rope came taut, shivered, and then snapped. The shark lay quietly for a little while on the surface and the old man watched him. Then he went down very slowly.

"He took about forty pounds," the old man said aloud. He took my harpoon too and all the rope, he thought, and now my fish bleeds again and there will be others.

He did not like to look at the fish anymore since he had been mutilated. When the fish had been hit it was as though he himself were hit.

But I killed the shark that hit my fish, he thought. And he was the biggest dentuso that I have ever seen. And God knows that I have seen big ones.

It was too good to last, he thought. I wish it had been a dream now and that I had never hooked the fish and was alone in bed on the newspapers.

"But man is not made for defeat," he said. "A man can be destroyed but not defeated." I am sorry that I killed the fish though, he thought. Now the bad time is coming and I do not even have the harpoon. The dentuso is cruel and able and strong and intelligent. But I was more intelligent that he was. Perhaps not, he thought. Perhaps I was only better armed.

"Don't think, old man," he said aloud. "Sail on this course and take it when it comes."

But I must think, he thought. Because it is all I have left. That and baseball. I wonder how the great DiMaggio would have liked the way I hit him in the brain? It was no great thing, he thought. Any man could do it. But do you think my hands were as great a handicap as the bone spurs? I cannot know. I never had anything wrong with my heel except the time the sting ray stung it when I stepped on him when swimming and paralyzed the lower leg and made the unbearable pain.

"Think about something cheerful, old man," he said. "Every minute now you are closer to home. You sail lighter for the loss of forty pounds."

He knew quite well the pattern of what could happen when he reached the inner part of the current. But there was

nothing to be done now.

"Yes there is," he said aloud. "I can lash my knife to the butt of one of the oars."

So he did that with the tiller under his arm and the sheet of the sail under his foot.

"Now," he said. "I am still an old man. But I am not unarmed."

The breeze was fresh now and he sailed on well. He watched only the forward part of the fish and some of his hope returned.

It is silly not to hope, he thought. Besides I believe it is a sin. Do not think about sin, he thought. There are enough problems now without sin. Also I have no understanding of it.

I have no understanding of it and I am not sure that I believe in it. Perhaps it was a sin to kill the fish. I suppose it was even though I did it to keep me alive and feed many people. But then everything is a sin. Do not think about sin. It is much too late for that and there are people who are paid to do it. Let them think about it. You were born to be a fisherman as the fish was born to be a fish. San Pedro was a fisherman as was the father of the great DiMaggio.

But he liked to think about all things that he was involved in and since there was nothing to read and he did not have a radio, he thought much and he kept on thinking about sin. You did not kill the fish only to keep alive and to sell for

food, he thought. You killed him for pride and because you are a fisherman. You loved him when he was alive and you loved him after. It you love him, it is not a sin to kill him. Or is it more?

"You think too much, old man," he said aloud.

But you enjoyed killing the dentuso, he thought. He lives on the live fish as you do. He is not a scavenger nor just a moving appetite as some sharks are. He is beautiful and noble and knows no fear of anything.

"I killed him in self-defense," the old man said aloud. "And I killed him well."

Besides, he thought, everything kills everything else in some way. Fishing kills me exactly as it keeps me alive. The boy keeps me alive, he thought. I must not deceive myself too much.

He leaned over the side and pulled loose a piece of the meat of the fish where the shark had cut him. He chewed it and noted its quality and its good taste. It was firm and juicy, like meat, but it was not red. There was no stringiness in it and he knew that it would bring the highest price in the market. But there was no way to keep its scent out of the water and the old man knew that a very bad time was coming.

The breeze was steady. It had backed a little further into the north-east and he knew that meant that it would not fall off. The old man looked ahead of him but he could see no sails nor could he see the hull nor the smoke of any ship.

There were only the flying fish that went up from his bow sailing away to either side and the yellow patches of gulf-weed. He could not even see a bird.

He had sailed for two hours, resting in the stern and sometimes chewing a bit of the meat from the marlin, trying to rest and to be strong, when he saw the first of the two sharks.

"Ay," he said aloud. There is no translation for this word and perhaps it is just a noise such as a man might make, involuntarily, feeling the nail go through his hands and into the wood.

"Galanos," he said aloud. He had seen the second fin now coming up behind the first and had identified them as shovel-nosed sharks by the brown, triangular fin and the sweeping movements of the tail. They had the scent and were excited and in the stupidity of their great hunger they were losing and finding the scent in their excitement. But they were closing all the time.

The old man made the sheet fast and jammed the tiller. Then he took up the oar with the knife lashed to it. He lifted it as lightly as he could because his hands rebelled at the pain. Then he opened and closed them on it lightly to loosen them. He closed them firmly so they would take the pain now and would not flinch and watched the sharks come. He could see their wide, flattened, shovel-pointed heads now and their white-tipped wide pectoral fins. They were hateful sharks, bad

smelling, scavengers as well as killers, and when they were hungry they would bite at an oar or the rudder of a boat. It was these sharks that would cut the turtles' legs and flippers off when the turtles were asleep on the surface, and they would hit a man in the water, if they were hungry, even if the man had no smell of fish blood nor of fish slime on him.

"Ay," the old man said. "Galanos. Come on, Galanos."

They came. But they did not come as the Mako had come. One turned and went out of sight under the skiff and the old man could feel the skiff shake as he jerked and pulled on the fish. The other watched the old man with his slitted yellow eyes and then came in fast with his half circle of jaws wide to hit the fish where he had already been bitten. The line

showed clearly on the top of his brown head and back where the brain joined the spinal cord and the old man drove the knife on the oar into the juncture, withdrew it, and drove it in again into the shark's yellow cat-like eyes. The shark let go of the fish and slid down, swallowing what he had taken as he died.

The skiff was still shaking with the destruction the other shark was doing to the fish and the old man let go the sheet so that the skiff would swing broadside and bring the shark out from under. When he saw the shark he leaned over the side and punched at him. He hit only meat and the hide was set hard and he barely got the knife in. The blow hurt not only his hands but his shoulder too. But the shark came up fast with his head out and the old man hit him squarely in the center of his flat-topped head as his nose came out of water and lay against the fish. The old man withdrew the blade and punched the shark exactly in the same spot again. He still hung to the fish with his jaws hooked and the old man stabbed him in his left eye. The shark still hung there.

"No?" the old man said and he drove the blade between the vertebrae and the brain. It was an easy shot now and he felt the cartilage sever. The old man reversed the oar and put the blade between the shark's jaws to open them. He twisted the blade and as the shark slid loose he said, "Go on, galano. Slide down a mile deep. Go see your friend, or maybe it's your mother."

The old man wiped the blade of his knife and laid down the oar. Then he found the sheet and the sail filled and he brought the skiff onto her course.

"They must have taken a quarter of him and of the best meat," he said aloud. "I wish it were a dream and that I had never hooked him. I'm sorry about it, fish. It makes everything wrong." He stopped and he did not want to look at the fish now. Drained of blood and awash he looked the colour of the silver backing of a mirror and his stripes still showed.

"I shouldn't have gone out so far, fish," he said. "Neither for you nor for me. I'm sorry, fish."

Now, he said to himself. Look to the lashing on the knife and see if it has been cut. Then get your hand in order because there still is more to come.

"I wish I had a stone for the knife," the old man said after he had checked the lashing on the oar butt. "I should have brought a stone." You should have brought many things, he thought. But you did not bring them, old man. Now is no time to think of what you do not have. Think of what you can do with what there is.

"You give me much good counsel," he said aloud. "I'm tired of it."

He held the tiller under his arm and soaked both his hands in the water as the skiff drove forward.

"God knows how much that last one took," he said. "But

she's much lighter now." He did not want to think of the mutilated under-side of the fish. He knew that each of the jerking bumps of the shark had been meat torn away and that the fish now made a trail for all sharks as wide as a highway through the sea.

He was a fish to keep a man all winter, he thought. Don't think of that. Just rest and try to get your hands in shape to defend what is left of him. The blood smell from my hands means nothing now with all that scent in the water. Besides they do not bleed much. There is nothing cut that means anything. The bleeding may keep the left from cramping.

What can I think of now? he thought. Nothing. I must think of nothing and wait for the next ones. I wish it had really been a dream, he thought. But who knows? It might have turned out well.

The next shark that came was a single shovel-nose. He came like a pig to the trough if a pig had a mouth so wide that you could put your head in it. The old man let him hit the fish and then drove the knife on the oar down into his brain. But the shark jerked backwards as he rolled and the knife blade snapped.

The old man settled himself to steer. He did not even watch the big shark sinking slowly in the water, showing first life-size, then small, then tiny. That always fascinated the old man. But he did not even watch it now.

"I have the gaff now," he said. "But it will do no good. I

have the two oars and the tiller and the short club."

Now they have beaten me, he thought. I am too old to club sharks to death. But I will try it as long as I have the oars and the short club and the tiller.

He put his hands in the water again to soak them. It was getting late in the afternoon and he saw nothing but the sea and the sky. There was more wind in the sky than there had been, and soon he hoped that he would see land.

"You're tired, old man," he said. "You're tired inside."

The sharks did not hit him again until just before sunset.

The old man saw the brown fins coming along the wide trail the fish must make in the water. They were not even quartering on the scent. They were headed straight for the skiff swimming side by side.

He jammed the tiller, made the sheet fast and reached under the stern for the club. It was an oar handle from a broken oar sawed off to about two and a half feet in length. He could only use it effectively with one hand because of the grip of the handle and he took good hold of it with his right hand, flexing his hand on it, as he watched the sharks come. They were both galanos.

I must let the first one get a good hold and hit him on the point of the nose or straight across the top of the head, he thought.

The two sharks closed together and as he saw the one nearest him open his jaws and sink them into the silver side

of the fish, he raised the club high and brought it down heavy and slamming onto the top of the shark's broad head. He felt the rubbery solidity as the club came down. But he felt the rigidity of bone too and he struck the shark once more hard across the point of the nose as he slid down from the fish.

The other shark had been in and out and now came in again with his jaws wide. The old man could see pieces of the meat of the fish spilling white from the corner of his jaws as he bumped the fish and closed his jaws. He swung at him and hit only the head and the shark looked at him and wrenched the meat loose. The old man swung the club down on him again as he slipped away to swallow and hit only the heavy solid rubberiness.

"Come on, galano," the old man said. "Come in again."

The shark came in a rush and the old man hit him as he shut his jaws. He hit him solidly and from as high up as he could raise the club. This time he felt the bone at the base of the brain and he hit him again in the same place while the shark tore the meat loose sluggishly and slid down from the fish.

The old man watched for him to come again but neither shark showed. Then he saw one on the surface swimming in circles. He did not see the fin of the other.

I could not expect to kill them, he thought. I could have in my time. But I have hurt them both badly and neither one can feel very good. If I could have used a bat with two hands

I could have killed the first one surely. Even now, he thought.

He did not want to look at the fish. He knew that half of him had been destroyed. The sun had gone down while he had been in the fight with the sharks.

"It will be dark soon," he said. "Then I should see the glow of Havana. If I am too far to the eastward I will see the lights of one of the new beaches."

I cannot be too far out now, he thought. I hope no one has been too worried. There is only the boy to worry, of course. But I am sure he would have confidence. Many of the older fishermen will worry. Many others too, he thought. I live in a good town.

He could not talk to the fish anymore because the fish had been ruined too badly. Then something came into his head.

"Half fish," he said. "Fish that you were. I am sorry that I went too far out. I ruined us both. But we have killed many sharks, you and I, and ruined many others. How many did you ever kill, old fish? You do not have that spear on your head for nothing."

He liked to think of the fish and what he could do to a shark if he were swimming free. I should have chopped the bill off to fight them with, he thought. But there was no hatchet and then there was no knife.

But if I had, and could have lashed it to an oar butt, what a weapon. Then we might have fought them together. What

will you do now if they come in the night? What can you do?

"Fight them," he said. "I'll fight them until I die."

But in the dark now and no glow showing and no lights and only the wind and the steady pull of the sail he felt that perhaps he was already dead. He put his two hands together and felt the palms. They were not dead and he could bring the pain of life by simply opening and closing them. He leaned his back against the stern and knew he was not dead. His shoulders told him.

I have all those prayers I promised if I caught the fish, he thought. But I am too tired to say them now. I better get the sack and put it over my shoulders.

He lay in the stern and steered and watched for the glow to come in the sky. I have half of him, he thought. Maybe I'll have the luck to bring the forward half in. I should have some luck. No, he said. You violated your luck when you went too far outside.

"Don't be silly," he said aloud. "And keep awake and steer. You may have much luck yet."

"I'd like to buy some if there's any place they sell it," he said.

What could I buy it with? he asked himself. Could I buy it with a lost harpoon and a broken knife and two bad hands?

"You might," he said. "You tried to buy it with eighty-four days at sea. They nearly sold it to you too."

I must not think nonsense, he thought. Luck is a thing

that comes in many forms and who can recognize her? I
would take some though in any form and pay what they
asked. I wish I could see the glow from the lights, he thought.
I wish too many things. But that is the thing I wish for now.
He tried to settle more comfortably to steer and from his pain
he knew he was not dead.

He saw the reflected glare of the lights of the city at
what must have been around ten o'clock at night. They were
only perceptible at first as the light is in the sky before the
moon rises. Then they were steady to see across the ocean
which was rough now with the increasing breeze. He steered
inside of the glow and he thought that now, soon, he must hit
the edge of the stream.

Now it is over, he thought. They will probably hit me
again. But what can a man do against them in the dark
without a weapon?

He was stiff and sore now and his wounds and all of the
strained parts of his body hurt with the cold of the night. I
hope I do not have to fight again, he thought. I hope so much
I do not have to fight again.

But by midnight he fought and this time he knew the
fight was useless. They came in a pack and he could only see
the lines in the water that their fins made and their
phosphorescence as they threw themselves on the fish. He
clubbed at heads and heard the jaws chop and the shaking of
the skiff as they took hold below. He clubbed desperately at

what he could only feel and hear and he felt something seize the club and it was gone.

He jerked the tiller free from the rudder and beat and chopped with it, holding it in both hands and driving it down again and again. But they were up to the bow now and driving in one after the other and together, tearing off the pieces of meat that showed glowing below the sea as they turned to come once more.

One came, finally, against the head itself and he knew that it was over. He swung the tiller across the shark's head where the jaws were caught in the heaviness of the fish's head which would not tear. He swung it once and twice and again. He heard the tiller break and he lunged at the shark with the splintered butt. He felt it go in and knowing it was sharp he drove it in again. The shark let go and rolled away. That was the last shark of the pack that came. There was nothing more for them to eat.

The old man could hardly breathe now and he felt a strange taste in his mouth. It was coppery and sweet and he was afraid of it for a moment. But there was not much of it.

He spat into the ocean and said, "Eat that, Galanos. And make a dream you've killed a man."

He knew he was beaten now finally and without remedy and he went back to the stern and found the jagged end of the tiller would fit in the slot of the rudder well enough for him to steer. He settled the sack around his shoulders and put

the skiff on her course. He sailed lightly now and he had no thoughts nor any feelings of any kind. He was past everything now and he sailed the skiff to make his home port as well and as intelligently as he could. In the night sharks hit the carcass as someone might pick up crumbs from the table. The old man paid no attention to them and did not pay any attention to anything except steering. He only noticed how lightly and how well the skiff sailed now there was no great weight beside her.

She's good, he thought. She is sound and not harmed in any way except for the tiller. That is easily replaced.

He could feel he was inside the current now and he could see the lights of the beach colonies along the shore. He knew where he was now and it was nothing to get home.

The wind is our friend, anyway, he thought. Then he added, sometimes. And the great sea with our friends and our enemies. And bed, he thought. Bed is my friend. Just bed, he thought. Bed will be a great thing. It is easy when you are beaten, he thought. I never knew how easy it was. And what beat you, he thought.

"Nothing," he said aloud. "I went out too far."

When he sailed into the little harbour the lights of the Terrace were out and he knew everyone was in bed. The breeze had risen steadily and was blowing strongly now. It was quiet in the harbour though and he sailed up onto the little patch of shingle below the rocks. There was no one to help

him so he pulled the boat up as far as he could. Then he stepped out and made her fast to a rock.

He unstepped the mast and furled the sail and tied it. Then he shouldered the mast and started to climb. It was then he knew the depth of his tiredness. He stopped for a moment and looked back and saw in the reflection from the street light the great tail of the fish standing up well behind the skiff's stern. He saw the white naked line of his backbone and the dark mass of the head with the projecting bill and all the nakedness between.

He started to climb again and at the top he fell and lay for some time with the mast across his shoulder. He tried to get up. But it was too difficult and he sat there with the mast on his shoulder and looked at the road. A cat passed on the far side going about its business and the old man watched it. Then he just watched the road.

Finally he put the mast down and stood up. He picked the mast up and put it on his shoulder and started up the road. He had to sit down five times before he reached his shack.

Inside the shack he leaned the mast against the wall. In the dark he found a water bottle and took a drink. Then he lay down on the bed. He pulled the blanket over his shoulders and then over his back and legs and he slept face down on the newspapers with his arms out straight and the palms of his hands up.

He was asleep when the boy looked in the door in the morning. It was blowing so hard that the drifting-boats would not be going out and the boy had slept late and then come to the old man's shack as he had come each morning. The boy saw that the old man was breathing and then he saw the old man's hands and he started to cry. He went out very quietly to go to bring some coffee and all the way down the road he was crying.

Many fishermen were around the skiff looking at what was lashed beside it and one was in the water, his trousers rolled up, measuring the skeleton with a length of line.

The boy did not go down. He had been there before and one of the fishermen was looking after the skiff for him.

"How is he?" one of the fishermen shouted.

"Sleeping," the boy called. He did not care that they saw him crying. "Let no one disturb him."

"He was eighteen feet from nose to tail," the fisherman who was measuring him called.

"I believe it," the boy said.

He went into the Terrace and asked for a can of coffee.

"Hot and with plenty of milk and sugar in it."

"Anything more?"

"No. Afterwards I will see what he can eat."

"What a fish it was," the proprietor said. "There has never been such a fish. Those were two fine fish you took yesterday too."

"Damn my fish," the boy said and he started to cry again.

"Do you want a drink of any kind?" the proprietor asked.

"No," the boy said. "Tell them not to bother Santiago. I'll be back."

"Tell him how sorry I am."

"Thanks," the boy said.

The boy carried the hot can of coffee up to the old man's shack and sat by him until he woke. Once it looked as though he were waking. But he had gone back into heavy sleep and the boy had gone across the road to borrow some wood to heat the coffee.

Finally the old man woke.

"Don't sit up," the boy said. "Drink this." He poured some of the coffee in a glass.

The old man took it and drank it.

"They beat me, Manolin," he said. "They truly beat me."

"He didn't beat you. Not the fish."

"No. Truly. It was afterwards."

"Pedrico is looking after the skiff and the gear. What do

you want done with the head?"

"Let Pedrico chop it up to use in fish traps."

"And the spear?"

"You keep it if you want it."

"I want it," the boy said. "Now we must make our plans about the other things."

"Did they search for me?"

"Of course. With coast guard and with planes."

"The ocean is very big and a skiff is small and hard to see," the old man said. He noticed how pleasant it was to have someone to talk to instead of speaking only to himself and to the sea. "I missed you," he said. "What did you catch?"

"One the first day. One the second and two the third."

"Very good."

"Now we fish together again."

"No. I am not lucky. I am not lucky anymore."

"The hell with luck," the boy said. "I'll bring the luck with me."

"What will your family say?"

"I do not care. I caught two yesterday. But we will fish together now for I still have much to learn."

"We must get a good killing lance and always have it on board. You can make the blade from a spring leaf from an old Ford. We can grind it in Guanabacoa. It should be sharp and not tempered so it will break. My knife broke."

"I'll get another knife and have the spring ground. How

many days of heavy brisa have we?"

"Maybe three. Maybe more."

"I will have everything in order," the boy said. "You get your hands well old man."

"I know how to care for them. In the night I spat something strange and felt something in my chest was broken."

"Get that well too," the boy said. "Lie down, old man, and I will bring you your clean shirt. And something to eat."

"Bring any of the papers of the time that I was gone," the old man said.

"You must get well fast for there is much that I can learn and you can teach me everything. How much did you suffer?"

"Plenty," the old man said.

"I'll bring the food and the papers," the boy said. "Rest well, old man. I will bring stuff from the drug-store for your hands."

"Don't forget to tell Pedrico the head is his."

"No. I will remember."

As the boy went out the door and down the worn coral rock road he was crying again.

That afternoon there was a party of tourists at the Terrace and looking down in the water among the empty beer cans and dead barracudas a woman saw a great long white spine with a huge tail at the end that lifted and swung with the tide while the east wind blew a heavy steady sea outside

the entrance to the harbour.

"What's that?" she asked a waiter and pointed to the long backbone of the great fish that was now just garbage waiting to go out with the tide.

"Tiburon," the waiter said, "Eshark." He was meaning to explain what had happened.

"I didn't know sharks had such handsome, beautifully formed tails."

"I didn't either," her male companion said.

Up the road, in his shack, the old man was sleeping again. He was still sleeping on his face and the boy was sitting by him watching him. The old man was dreaming about the lions.

The end.

國家圖書館出版品預行編目資料

老人與海 ／ 恩尼斯特·海明威（Ernest Hemingway）
作 ； 曾銘祥、Raymond Sheppard繪 ； 李毓昭譯. ―
二版. ― 臺中市 ： 晨星, 2020.12
　面； 公分. ― （愛藏本；106）
中英雙語典藏版
譯自：The Old Man and the Sea
ISBN 978-986-5529-86-4（精裝）

874.57　　　　　　　　　　　　　　　109017607

愛藏本：106

老人與海（中英雙語典藏版）
The Old Man and the Sea

作者｜恩尼斯特·海明威（Ernest Hemingway）
繪者｜曾銘祥、Raymond Sheppard
譯者｜李毓昭

責任編輯｜呂曉婕、謝宜真
封面設計｜鐘文君
文字校潤｜呂曉婕、謝宜真

創 辦 人｜陳銘民
發 行 所｜晨星出版有限公司
　　　　　台中市 407 工業區 30 路 1 號 1 樓
　　　　　TEL:(04)23595820 FAX:(04)23550581
　　　　　http://star.morningstar.com.tw
　　　　　行政院新聞局局版台業字第 2500 號
法律顧問｜陳思成律師
服務專線｜ TEL:（02）23672044 /（04）23595819#212
傳真專線｜ FAX:（02）23635741 /（04）23595493
讀者信箱｜ service@morningstar.com.tw
網路書店｜ http://www.morningstar.com.tw
郵政劃撥｜ 15060393（知己圖書股份有限公司）

印刷｜上好印刷股份有限公司

初版日期｜ 2003 年 06 月 30 日
二版二刷｜ 2022 年 09 月 20 日
定價｜新台幣 250 元
ISBN 978-986-5529-86-4

填寫線上回函，立刻享有
晨星網路書店50元購書金